WILL,

the Passenger Delaying Flight ...

WILL,

the Passenger Delaying Flight ...

BARBARA ADAIR

Published in 2020 by Modjaji Books
www.modjajibooks.co.za

© Barbara Adair

Edited by Alison Lowry
Cover artwork by Diane Swartzberg
Cover design by Monique Cleghorn
Typesetting Andy Thesen
Set in Minion Pro

ISBN print: 978-1-928-215-94-3
ebook: 978-1-928-215-95-0

This book was written for you

VOLKER WALKS SLOWLY, and sometimes he walks fast, across the airport concourse, his speed, and the way he moves, depends upon the speed of the other people who also walk there, some walk fast, they almost run, as if they have somewhere to be, others meander, wander, as if they have no purpose, no reason, *do we all have no reason, I am born and I die and the reason for being in this airport is that I am alive, I am alive so I may as well be in this airport, walking.* Volker has just arrived at Charles de Gaulle airport after a short flight, the journey from Frankfurt to Paris takes one hour and fifteen minutes. Now he walks, sometimes as if he has a purpose, other times as if he does not. He remembers.

I am alone.[1]

The airline is Lufthansa, it is German.[2] *Streamlined, almost*

1. All good writers borrow; all remarkable writers steal. Some of these words and lines are stolen from others. The others that come to mind here are Will Self, Paul Bowles, Jane Bowles, Alexander Trocchi, Stewart Home, Peter Beard, Italo Calvino, Jorge Luis Borges, U2, Michel Butor, Ann Quin and Alain Robbe-Grillet. 'I am alone' is from the book *The Erasers* (or is it *In the Labyrinth?*) by Robbe-Grillet. This text, however, does not form part of novels known as the New Novel, the *Nouveau Roman*. This is a modernist novel, the subjective that does not try to be objective.

2. Flying is a metaphor for ecstasy. Flying is unempirical, so in a society of empiricism flying is not flying for it is referred to only in aeronautical terms (unless you are Antoine de Saint-Exupéry). Lufthansa, the German national carrier, does fly, but not ecstatically; it flies aerodynamically and profitably. It is German. Everything about it is grounded in reality. There is only the empirical and the pragmatic.

perfect for Germany can never not be perfect though her history is so bad, does this mean that I am bad, evil, does evil exist without good? Where does Goethe fit into all of this, or Schiller, for that matter, maybe the Ride of the Valkyries[3] *will allow us into a heaven, Thor's heaven.* The C-class section of the Boeing 747 is elongated, semi-dark, it stretches in front of Volker, *the aisle is so long I can barely see the end of it, a Boeing is a measurement of the end of the world, I see the end of the world, I am so small, a miniature version of a man, an ant, a velveteen rabbit,*[4] *I can never be real.* On either side of him are

---

a. Lufthansa is the world's fourth-largest airline in terms of passenger numbers.
b. These passengers travel to a variety of destinations in that the airline operates services to 18 domestic destinations, that is, destinations in Germany, and 203 international destinations spread over 78 countries. These countries cross continents: Africa, North and South America, Asia and Europe.
c. Lufthansa, together with myriad partners, services around 410 destinations.
d. The airline owns over 710 aircraft, including the Boeing 747 that Volker is in, and, when combined with its subsidiaries, it has the second-largest passenger airline fleet in the world.
e. Lufthansa's registered office and corporate headquarters are in Deutz.
f. The main traffic centre is in Frankfurt, with a second hub in Munich.
g. Lufthansa flies to Windhoek, as Namibia is a favourite tourist destination for hungry German hunters.
h. Should you want to read anything further about this airline log in to Wikipedia.

3.   Goethe, a German writer, and Schiller, a German philosopher, are famous. Goethe loved the more famous Wagner, a German composer, who wrote the four operas that make up *Der Ring des Nibelungen*. *The Ride of the Valkyries* is in the second of these four operas and was featured in the movie *Apocalypse Now* as the Americans napalmed a small village in Vietnam.

4.   *The Velveteen Rabbit*, also entitled *How Toys Become Real*, is a children's novel written by Margery Williams and illustrated by William Nicholson. The book is about a toy rabbit made of velveteen that is given as a Christmas present to a young boy, but then is neglected by him for better, more exciting toys. The velveteen rabbit is told how he can become real by the

seats, there are two sets of seats, one to the right and one to the left, three seats in each set, in each set the seats are joined together at the armrests. On the cloth cover of the armrest that is next to him but for one seat, there is a hole, it is a burn, the edges are black, a cigarette burned the material some time ago when smoking was still permitted on aeroplanes, the edges are frayed. *Remember the movie Henry and June, the cigarette smoke that curls from the sides of Uma Thurman's lips, June's mouth is sexy, Henry's too, but June's? Remember when Anaïs watched the two women have sex; they looked like her and June. Why were cigarettes banned on aeroplanes? I am breathing, breathing in air and I do not care for air.* Volker wants to smoke, the burned patch, *smoke-filled aeroplanes and scratchy eyes when the flight is a long flight, some East German insomniac chain smokers drinking whiskey. A sign, ON then OFF ... SMOKING/NO SMOKING; where is that fucking sign?*[5]

---

wisest toy in the nursery. To become real a toy must be adored and loved by the child who owns him (love and ownership go hand in hand). The velveteen rabbit is overwhelmed by this; however, he is also sad as his chances of achieving reality are minimal. One night, after the young boy has lost his treasured china dog, he is made to feel better by the velveteen rabbit. The young boy then comes down with scarlet fever. In order that he recover fully he is sent on a trip to the coast. He is unhappy and does not want to go; he wants to remain in his home. He is soothed when he is given a stuffed rabbit that is of a better quality than the velveteen rabbit; the velveteen rabbit is replaced, and must be burned with all of the other toys that harbour the dangerous scarlet fever virus. Then the velveteen rabbit is magically transformed into a living rabbit by a fairy so as to spare him from this fiery fate. He became the young boy's best and most adored toy after all. So the velveteen rabbit achieved real greatness.

5.   Paul Bowles wrote: I used to think that life was a thing that kept gaining impetus. It would get richer and deeper each year. I keep learning, getting wiser, going further into the truth. And now I know that it's not like that. It's more like smoking a cigarette. The first few puffs, it tastes wonderful and I never think of it ever being used up. Then I begin to take it for granted. And suddenly I realise that it is almost burnt down to the end, my fingers burn. And then I am conscious of a bitter taste. And I think that if I am always conscious of this unpleasant disagreeable bitter

Volker sits on the third seat at the end of the row of seats, he is close to the window. A man wearing a blue tracksuit and a white T-shirt sits next to him, he is a large man, he is sweating and drinking water, many bottles of water, on the pocket of his T-shirt are the words 'Princeton Alumni'. *What is he, a professor, a sought-after intellect, I can hear the sound of water following the edges of his throat, is the professor crying?* The man in the blue tracksuit looks resolutely at the book he holds, but the reading light is not turned on, it is off, it is dark, every few minutes he lifts his head and looks forward, into the distance, which only just reaches to the far end of the aeroplane, then he turns his head a fraction to the left and looks out of the window, he appears to be thinking. *Nothing is further from self-knowledge than introspection, wisdom is remote, wisdom is intellect …*

CHARLES GRAYSON SMITH, Junior,[6] is a traveller. This is what he now calls himself as he is aware that in the world it is necessary to call oneself something for labels give meaning to the other otherwise meaningless. It is important to have an identity. The word traveller has connotations of doing something, and to be doing something, to be busy, is important, for to do nothing is considered to be both lazy and dangerous. He has not always been a traveller. Once, not that long ago, a few years, he was a professor of economics at Harvard.

---

taste I should give up smoking. And then I realise that living is a habit, like smoking. I always say I am going to give it up, but I just go right on living.

6.   While the names of some real persons are used for characters in the text, these characters appear in a fictionalised setting. There is no intention to suggest that they bear any other than the most superficial similarity to actual people bearing the same names. Any other resemblance to living people is entirely unintended. But don't invest in any of these characters; they will come into your life, and they will go from it, as quickly as the people who walk and run past you in an airport.

This university is considered to be the best in the Ivy League category. Whether it is or not, this is not necessary to debate. All we need to agree on is that this university is in America, and because America defines the world, the only world, it is an illustrious university. But unfortunately his life took a downward spiral. He was accused of plagiarism. The woman, the student, who accused him – who can judge her motivation? Was it because he had spurned her sexually – of course he did, he was a homosexual – or was it because she was vindictive, he never gave her very high grades, her work was not interesting or well thought through. Or was it because he really did copy the work of another?

Charles Junior comes from the distinguished, famous some would say, Smith family. His father, Charles Grayson Smith, Senior, is a very successful businessman and a celebrity, within America, that is, actually just Texas, and to be more specific, Houston. With some luck, and a lot of money he borrowed from the Chase Manhattan Bank, before it went under and was rescued by the taxpayer, he paid this money back. In hindsight he probably did not have to and so would be wealthier than he is; his success came from oil exploration. He discovered an enormous oil deposit on the farm of an elderly man and woman. This farm was approximately one hundred and fifty miles south of Houston. He bought the farm from them for a handsome figure, and once he had paid the money to them they were able to buy a small house in a secure development somewhere safer. It is never safe to live on a smallholding.

Charles Senior knocked down the farmhouse and drilled deep. He found oil and made a fortune. This fortune was enough to send his children to the best universities, that is the ones who wanted to go to university. The younger son, Bert, did not, he preferred the bohemianism of art college, while the two older siblings, Charles Junior and his sister Sue attended Houston University. They then went on to other more notable institutions. Fortunately for Charles Senior the payment of their education paid off, not because his children were brilliant but because they managed to do fairly well, and because Charles Senior always donated handsomely to the institutions they attended. Soon after graduating from Houston Charles Senior paid for Charles Junior's postgraduate studies at the University of Southern California, sometimes known as the University of Spoilt Children. This was because, despite Charles Senior's protestations, Charles Junior wanted to leave Texas to experience the exuberance and excitement of what he perceived to be the anti-establishment environment in California.

During his time in Los Angeles he experimented with anti-Vietnam war protests and drugs, mostly LSD, but at the same time kept his head and graduated in economics, for he knew that there was little future in hallucinations and folk music, unless you were Patti Smith or Joan Baez. After this he left the west coast and went east to Boston. He was accepted at Harvard University as here, once again, his tuition was paid for by the ever-increasing wealth of Charles Senior.

At Harvard there was not a lot to distract him, and his father made a large donation to the economics library so he excelled, in fact he graduated cum laude, and was at once offered a post as a junior lecturer in the economics department. He worked in the department for twenty years; soon he was a senior lecturer, then more senior, eventually a professor and tipped to be head of the department. His career was unblemished. He was frequently cited in major journals, his students enjoyed the way he presented his classes, they were more clownish than intellectual for Charles was naturally funny, and yet they also provoked a critical analysis of late capitalism in America (and elsewhere, although there is no elsewhere). He always made them consider other systems of economic development, not merely the accumulation of wealth but, possibly, they could think about an accumulation of satisfaction. They never did.

Unfortunately for Charles Junior his career came to an abrupt end. He wrote an article for the *Harvard Journal of Economic Reform* (HJER). It was published and acclaimed; people talked about it in the hallways and even in the high-rise buildings of New York City. It established a model for development that was different to the model proffered, and sold, by the IMF; it challenged and irritated, people loathed it or loved it. The student who accused him, who came from somewhere in the Midwest, was extremely adept at Google searches – what else is there to do in the Midwest where the only world without corn fields is on the computer – and she found an article written by an obscure sociologist, Feodor Raskolnikov, who lived, he was now dead, in what was previously known as Leningrad in the Soviet Union. For a long time the article was unavailable to most English-speaking people, but, with the advent of Google Translate, it could now be read by everyone. Exact words, even phrases, were replicated without shame in the article that Charles Junior had written. Plagiarism is a heinous sin in the academic world, in America immense pride is taken in being an individual, work must always be new and unique. So no matter how much Charles Junior argued that no thought is new and that all works are a tapestry of other writings, or that there is no such thing as originality, some people just do the same thing better than others, Barthes is not fashionable, he never really was in the economic sphere, so no one listened. Most free-thinking economists were also outraged that they could be taken in by someone from a formerly communist country. Charles Junior, in his own defence, put forward another translation of the work. This translation was prepared by a linguist who was not employed at Harvard but at Princeton. This translation was very different to the one by Google Translate, but in the end who can doubt Google. So Charles Junior was called before a disciplinary committee and after lengthy debates as to his unblemished career and how much he had contributed to the university it was decided to let him go. He was fired. There were many protests calling for his dismissal, as there were many that called for his reinstatement, but by this time Charles Junior knew that he had had enough. He now wanted to travel the world so he agreed to resign, so as not to leave ignominiously. In addition to his pension, and this was large as he had been working at the university for twenty years, he also received a handsome package. As he was well connected in the economic world, he had made many friends, and few enemies; he knew that in a society where wealth equals power and power equals influence it was better to keep in with all of the above for they might be needed sometime in the future. His package and his pension is therefore extremely well invested. Now he is rather well off, not rich as is Charles Senior, who is very rich, just well off. Also, of this he is well aware, that when his father died his wealth would be bequeathed to him, and his two siblings.

Charles Junior has a bestselling crime book in his hands, but he is not reading it, he is staring into the dark and wondering his future destination. He is flying to Paris, from there he will catch a train to Latvia because he wants to explore what was formally the Soviet Union, he believes that he has some spiritual connection to the remnants of communism, what it is he does not know, and from there he will move on to Mongolia, Ulan Bator has always been somewhere he would like to spend a birthday and soon he will be sixty. He also likes the Mongol look, flat faces and hungry slanting eyes. He may find a Mongolian bride there if he is able, a male bride for he has always, despite being in a liberal environment and hiding his homosexual proclivity, desired young Asian men. He wears a Princeton T-shirt because, although he never attended Princeton, it was given to him by the linguist who did the translation in his defence, so the T-shirt has some sentimental value. When he gave it to Charles Junior he had a wry expression and said, no more Harvard, old boy. Charles Junior does not much like the T-shirt but it is comfortable and a very easy shirt to wear while flying. In the past, when he was a well-known economist, he wore suits and red ties, now he wears a pair of blue tracksuit pants.

A PRINCETON ALUMNUS, *huff.* Volker looks ahead, a woman in a blue uniform is walking down the centre aisle of the aeroplane, as he watches her she moves towards him, *a man squeezes a woman out of a tube of toothpaste, women, their only role is to clean my teeth,* she walks slowly down the stretched-out aisle, Volker reaches between his legs and brushes his cock as he leans into his bag, he does not look inside it, he finds his glasses by touch and puts them on, he hooks the black plastic arms over his ears, his eyes are surrounded by black frames, plain black frames, there are no sparkling stones that glitter in them. The glasses surround his eyes, *my badge of safety. I am going nowhere, going nowhere, where am I going, going nowhere, and going, movement, and moving, disappearing. Do I have a secret that I want to hide?* The woman who walks at a steady pace down the aisle has sparkling stones glittering on the edges of her glasses, each time she walks under a spotlight, the spotlight turns ON and OFF as the light reflects off the rhinestones of the glasses, Volker reaches up, there is a switch in the aeroplane cabin ceiling, it may be turned ON or OFF depending on the needs of the passenger who sits in that seat, it is a swivel light, the direction the light bulb faces is any direction, Volker reaches up and turns on the light, her glasses flicker in each of the light bulbs, they reflect the blue sky above the mechanical engine, *trolley dolly, tart with a cart.* The woman pushes a cart. *I wish I did not have to do this work, if only I could just fuck for money, I hate to be polite, it annoys me, the higher I soar the smaller I am to those who cannot fly, but I cannot fly, I am a waitress in the sky, I am only polite, I can only be polite for if I am not I will never be able to wish.* She is the air hostess,[7] the flight attendant, *an air hostess, a trolley dolly, a tart behind a cart.* At each seat she stops and hands a white piece of cloth to the passenger who sits in that seat, the cloth is be used to wipe dirty hands, *dirty faces, dirty minds,* with a chemical cleaning agent, *why do I incessantly ask the meaning of this work, the meaning of life when the answer is so obvious ...*

CLAUDINE HAS VERY white teeth, they are stained by a tooth whitener, an ersatz replication of Colgate, and the skin on the underside of her bare arms is dappled, the lighting of the aeroplane, or possibly, cellulite. She prefers to think that it is the lighting of the aeroplane.

Claudine often wonders why she cannot be called Claudette, the name seems to have a bolder ring to it, the name Claudine suits a cat rather than a woman but unfortunately when it came to recording her name in her identification papers the autocratic machinery of the German government made a mistake. There was nothing she could do about it.

Claudine is thirty, almost past the sell-by date for an air hostess, or is it flight attendant, but she can probably make it through the next few years, these days it is frowned upon to discriminate against the elderly. So, although the airlines do not like employing older people, especially as flight attendants, be they men or women, for no one actually likes

---

7. Air hostesses are very often associated with pornography and waitressing. Sometimes they are good performers, good pornography is classic, and sometimes they are noted for their exceptional service, the glamour and skill of a movie star. But they also have skills, waitressing skills; it is difficult to move the trolleys in such a small space; it is hard work handing out cellophane-wrapped food parcels to more than 500 people. And they do know how to administer a little first aid. The association with pornography is an odious stereotype; these numerous air hostess fantasies are alarming.

Do you also want to fuck the air hostess?

employing the old, Claudine is still employed. However, the airline, Lufthansa, employs her for other reasons, or rather it has kept her in their employ and promoted her.

Charles Junior looks at Claudine. He notices her large hands, far too large for a woman, and thinks of the aphorism, big hands, big dick. However, he thinks no further of this after a momentary contemplation because he enjoys the bodies of men. And while Claudine may have the hands of the man of his dreams, she is, unfortunately, not a man.

Claudine used to be part of the Lufthansa ground staff, the luckless ones who sit behind desks and attend to the needs of passengers who have no air ticket, or want to change their air ticket, or some other such need that requires attendance. The ground staff are also those behind the desks at check-in. Ground staff are often harassed, bullied and even on occasion assaulted, by irate passengers who have too much luggage, or their luggage weighs too much, or they are late, or they want to take a truck aboard the aeroplane as hand luggage. Sometimes they get angry when the ground staff take away their knives, for they take away all knives, even small portable penknives, or their cigarette lighters. Once she, Claudine that is, or was it he, she can't remember, took away a gold Cartier lighter, he pocketed it before anyone knew it, before they noticed that he did not put it in the container for confiscated items. Claudine knew a designer lighter when it was in front of him.

Claudine had been promoted to flight attendant when he had become a she, as previously she was he; this is why she cannot remember if it was he or she who took the Cartier lighter. She still has it and she likes to take it out in a smart restaurant. Claudine, previously known as Claude, was promoted by Lufthansa as part of their forward-thinking advertising campaign; they wanted to show the world that this airline, although it is German and therefore has a suspect past, had put all prejudice and bigotry behind them. They now employ transsexuals, and, of course, Jews.

Luckily, Claude was experiencing extreme emotional challenges at the right time, the time when Lufthansa decided to show the world that this was an airline that cared. Claude had taken an indefinite leave of absence from the airline, sick leave, it was lengthy, he had also accumulated substantial vacation leave and so had applied to take this too. All of this leave was taken so that he could undergo surgery and become what he most dreamed of being, a woman. However, just before he was due to take his leave he was assaulted by a passenger who, Claude insisted, could not take his miniature Doberman onto the aircraft. It was the policy of the airline to allow no animals in the passenger sections of the aircraft, all personal pets had to be put in the cargo hold. Exceptions were only made for celebrities who travelled First Class, or politicians, Angela Merkel regularly travelled with her miniature Alsatian, although she travelled Economy Class to indicate that she was, and always will be, one of the people. She is, after all, East German. The passenger, a wholly manly man, was also keen to try out his new pastime, which was to have blow jobs on the side, so when he had tried to pick Claude up and had been refused he was even more outraged. So this effrontery, the refusal to give him a blow job in the toilet stall close to the check-in counter and the callous refusal to allow his dog to board the aeroplane, caused the man to push his blond hair from his blue eyes, he was very Aryan, and to punch Claude in the face. When Claude was interviewed about the assault, and it was agreed that he would not press charges, even though his nose was broken, but the man who assaulted him was a football player, a minor one, he was often on the benches, at Bayern München, it was revealed that Claude was about to take a lengthy period of leave. The human resources manager cajoled Claude into revealing that he was about to transition. The airline was delighted. This, the employment of a transsexual, would sit well with their advertising campaign, so they generously paid for all Claude's surgery, including the surgery that was needed to reconstruct his broken nose, and allowed him as much time as it took to recover. It was, after all, not a large amount of money for a large profitable corporation. After all this Claude returned to work as Claudine and, more than this, she would work far away from the ground and passengers who punched her, or him, and take to the air. Here, as she later found out, there were other problems, like blow jobs in even smaller toilet stalls, but this she would have to deal with as the tips were so much better than those on the ground.

So now she was earning more and flying round the world, well not around the world, rather more locally, around Europe. She had not yet been to the Americas or to Africa, although she had met a few Americans, those who recognised her for who and what she was, a trans-woman. One of the Americans, Sue, whom she had met some while ago, even promised to take care of her if she ever came to America, or so Claudine believed, she hoped, that she would get there soon. She was the face of the airline's accommodating liberalism campaign and she would, she believed, she hoped, get anything.

Unfortunately for Claudine, time passes and soon it was no longer fashionable to be a transsexual, and so the airline considered her only as another flight attendant, nothing more and nothing less. She is no longer the Christine Jorgensen[8] of the German airwaves, now she is just a flight attendant. And what with the economic recession coming in and cuts in staff looming there is a possibility that she could be retrenched, let go, as it is euphemistically said, for she is a newly employed

---

8. Christine Jorgensen was an American GI who, in 1951, underwent a transition from male to female. She then worked as an actress and nightclub entertainer. In 1959, when she wanted to marry, she was unable to do so as she was, in terms of all state documentation, a man. She is known to have said that she gave the sexual revolution 'a good swift kick in the pants'. And she was immortalised in a picture by Andy Warhol, Shoes (Christine Jorgenson), 1956, collaged metal leaf and embossed foil with ink on paper.

flight attendant. The downside of her transformation, once she became Claudine and was no longer Claude, was that she had to start as a new employee, consequently she had not worked for the airline for a long time.

There are certain occurrences in life which you win and some which you lose. Claudine likes her new body, but she finds it extremely difficult to find a boyfriend. And soon she may be unemployed. And she is forced to wear a scarf to cover her protruding Adam's apple, she hates this. Once, when she took off her scarf because the aircraft air-conditioning was not switched on and she felt extremely hot, a number of passengers began to complain that there was a circus freak on board. The only person who stood up for her was not very tall, an American person with dwarfism, in a clown costume. He insisted that there was nothing at all wrong with being a freak, and those who worked in a circuses, even though she worked for a large airline and didn't understand the circus reference, were legitimately employed even though they, most of the time, could not get any other job.

Charles Junior looks at Claudine again. He rather likes this large-handed handsome woman, and he can't imagine why. If only she were a man.

EACH TIME THE woman stops she reaches out and takes the piece of cleaning material and hands it to a passenger, *a mechanical arm reaches out, at each stop a mechanical arm appears, disappears.* The air hostess has rhinestones in her glasses, they surround her face, she wears a scarf around her neck and a blue uniform with the picture of a bird[9] on it that is drawn tightly across her breasts, tight and slightly open. Volker looks at her breasts, *a red nipple, I can rip this blue dress off, I can open her legs, I can smell her, can I make*

9.   The Lufthansa logo is a crane in flight, a bird that seldom flies in flight, as it is unable to fly outside the circle. It was designed by the surrealist Otto Firle.

her lick my boots, as she leans forward to give him a piece of cleaning material. She moves past him and he reaches out to take the material. The air hostess smiles at him, or at the man in the blue tracksuit with the words Princeton Alumni on his T-shirt, who sits next to him, or at a passenger in front of him, or the one behind, her smile is fixed and painted, painted red and does not move, *my mouth is a photograph, my lips are tired, how much can I earn tonight, how many times must I smile, open my lips, give a blow job?* After Volker cleans his hands with the chemical-covered cloth he puts his left hand into the seat pocket in front of him, the pocket is on the back of the seat that is directly ahead of him, it is low, he does not even have to stretch his arm out because the seat in front of him has been lowered, not lowered so as to make a bed as he is seated in Economy Class where there are no such things as beds, but low enough so that his knees touch the seat. He moves them to reach into the pocket, *if only I could travel in Business Class, more comfortable.* There is a plastic pamphlet in the pocket, paper covered in plastic, laminated so as not to tear easily, for it is lifted up and looked at by many people, and a magazine, *if only I could work in Business Class, better tips, less work, more time to assess the johns, guess I'll get there someday, someday over the rainbow, but I fear the rainbow.* In the magazine there is a picture of a German author, Max Frisch, and next to it a review of his book *Homo Faber.* Max Frisch is dead, *can I ever control my destiny …*

CLAUDINE STARES OUT of the window and has the same fantasy that she always has. One day she will decide that she has had enough of being an air hostess, and on a 26 December, her birthday, she will leave. She often talks about her fantasies to Jim or, as he likes to call himself, Peter, the older man with the grey-blond hair who works in the curio shop. He understands her need for adventure, he tells many fantastical stories himself, stories about models and Africa and being maimed by an elephant, which is why he is in this shop now, for he can no longer see as well as he used to, the elephant stabbed his eyes. Jim/Peter likes to talk about his adventures, and Claudine likes to listen for she too wants to leave the comfort of being a flight attendant.

There is no right time to leave so her birthday will be as right a time as any. Claudine imagines that she will place a few things in a bag, one or two pieces of underwear, a change of trousers, one extra shirt, and face cream (face cream is extremely important because hormones do interesting things to the skin). The bag, as it does not have many things in it, will be small, compact and light. She will catch a train to the airport and walk to the departures section; she will look at the lighted board that indicates what flights go where. She will take out her passport, she will look at the document, she does have a visa, it was given to her a few years ago but it is still valid, for the United States of America, how trusting they are, a visa for ten years.

And Claudine knows someone in America. And Jim/Peter says that he knows many people there. Claudine knows Susan Grayson Smith, she met her only once, this was on a flight several months, or is it years, ago, from Frankfurt to Paris. Susan was in Business Class and sometimes Claudine worked this section on the local European flights. They had begun a conversation as Sue, as Claudine now likes to call her, suffered from dry parched skin so was always calling the flight attendant for water, and always putting more cream on her very smooth skin. And Claudine was sure that Sue knew that she was a trans woman, Sue looked like a lesbian and so the word trans would be in her vocabulary. Sue told Claudine, who was always interested in face creams, that she had invented a miracle cream that prevented wrinkles, or at least minimised them. This was why she could afford to fly Business Class. She was a chemist and knew all about the workings of obscure molecules and chemicals. She knew that the ageing process could not be stopped, but it could be ameliorated. So, being clever, she patented her creation and sold it for an exceptionally large sum of money to Estée Lauder, one of the biggest cosmetics companies in the United States. Now she could do any chemical experiments she wanted to do. But as Claudine, and possibly the rest of the world knows, money begets money, and so in time Sue built up a good reputation in the cosmetics industry and was soon asked by many companies for different formulae which would do much the same thing as the first one did. She was in fact travelling to Paris, from there she would catch a train to Nice to meet a representative of Yves St Laurent who was holidaying in Juan Les Pins. Claudine is certain that Sue likes her, Claudine believes she likes her masculine femininity. She suspects that Sue is aware that she is trans, and, as a chemist, must be very impressed by the smoothness of her skin. There is not even a hint of stubble.

In her thoughts Claudine will look at the board again and, for a long time, she will read the city words. She will walk to the ticket sales desk and ask when the next flight to Atlanta in the United States is and whether there are any seats left on it. The next flight is a flight that flies via Turkey and there is a seat available, a seat in the smoking section, Turkish Airlines is the only airline where it is possible to smoke on board. She will then wonder if she can inhale smoke for ten hours and will decide that she can, she is a smoker anyway, and can show off her gold Cartier lighter. Then she thinks that she cannot go to Atlanta as she has very little money, permission only to visit not to stay indefinitely and work, and the United States is expensive. But then she will think, oh what the hell, and I know Sue Grayson Smith, she will definitely remember me, she may even have had a small crush on me, and she can't live far away, she lives in San Francisco. So Claudine will then buy a ticket, it is more expensive than she anticipates but none the less today is the day that she is leaving. She knows that before contacting Sue she will be able to manage financially for at least a few months. She can go to Las Vegas, fade into the desert, work in a nightclub, a steakhouse, or become a caretaker, a caregiver, a writer.

Yes, today, today is the day she will leave; time to start anew, get a new name, try another brand of cigarettes, become a vegetarian. In her mind the sound system calls out, Turkish Airlines Flight 5365 to Istanbul and Atlanta, boarding at Gate 4, boarding gate will close in twenty minutes. She will get up, may as well get to the boarding gate early, no need to give the ground staff more work should she be late. She will pick up her bag and walk to Gate 4. She will hand her boarding card to the good-looking, or is he pretty, man at the counter. She will be directed to a tunnel that leads her into the aeroplane. She will walk this familiar tunnel and step into the aeroplane, then she will climb some stairs, her seat is at the top of the aeroplane, and she will walk down the middle aisle. She will find her seat, sit down, fasten her seat-belt, listen assiduously to the airline steward mouth the safety instructions, pick up the in-flight magazine and begin to read of stars in the southern hemisphere, astronomers believe that there are many more interesting stars that are visible in the south. She imagines looking at the stars in the south from the north and smiles; she knows that she has made the right decision.

And Sue – the American man who is seated next to the German on this flight and who stares at her lasciviously even though he looks slightly effeminate, she noticed how he minced when he went to the toilet, the man who is wearing the T-shirt that says Princeton Alumni, looks a lot like her – will meet her somewhere and they will become new best friends.

But Claudine will not do any of this. Instead, in about two hours, she will walk into Charles de Gaulle airport, as she always does, and take a rest in the Business Class lounge, as she always does, for she has a long time to wait before she boards the domestic flight that will take her back home to Frankfurt. She will need to rest. She will need to watch nothing at all, and in the Business Class lounge there is nothing at all to watch.

I FEAR THE *future, I fear it because I have a future, a future to loiter in, a future where I will remain for no obvious reason.* The pamphlet is covered in writing; there are also red and blue diagrams on it, pictures of the aeroplane, the safety instructions. Should there be a sudden loss of air pressure oxygen masks will fall automatically downwards, always help the passenger next to you to place the mask over his or her face, place it tightly. The words are pictures of the tape recording that was played before the flight took off, a written tape recording. The cloth of the seat pocket has the airline carrier logo on it, a bird encircled in blue, the pocket is torn at the one corner, it has been opened so many times that the cotton used to sew up the edges has given way to the pressure, it hangs downwards, not so much so that what is in the pocket falls out, but it hangs down anyway, it brushes Volker's knee, *I can feel her hand move on my leg, upwards, on the inside of my thigh.* There is also a magazine in the pocket, an airline magazine. Volker picks up the plastic pamphlet. In addition to safety instructions, it sets out some information related to the aeroplane, Boeing 747-400: We own forty of these craft, but soon they will be discarded and replaced by a newer and more efficient aeroplane, the A380. This airline believes in safety. Volker looks around him, at the man in the white T-shirt who sits next to him, at the air hostess, *will I die on this aeroplane that is to be discarded, will I be discarded, will I be a part of a tragedy, tragedy is lush, the word is lissome, in my tragedy I will renounce myself, my need to contribute to the world's largesse for I am indifferent to intimacy, I will die in this indifferent sky for this aeroplane is unwanted; old and unusable, I am flying to somewhere, as I took off from the ground somewhere in Germany I elevated myself above the trivialities of that life, now I must find a new understanding, I have to search for I must find, but all I find is more trivia.* As he scans the pamphlet the aeroplane descends at a faster rate, it began its descent sometime earlier, but then the movement was imperceptible, the nose pointed downward just a fraction, this he did not know, could not know, it is knowledge known only to those who know they are not far from Paris, or those who know about aircraft and can feel the slight change in heading, *I know, I know, or do I know because I am certain of the time, the time it takes to come to the ground, I know because I know that today is the same as yesterday, as it will be tomorrow.* He holds the plastic paper in front of his eyes; the Boeing 747-400 can take up to two hundred and seventy-nine passengers in Economy Class. Volker puts the plastic pamphlet back into the pocket, *what if all the passengers are travelling in a pair,* which is torn in the one corner and he takes out the airline magazine. On the cover is a picture, *how faithful am I, how credible can I be,* a picture of the banks of the Rhine, *rhine-stones glitter in the water,* it could be another river, *it is another river for all rivers look the same,* but it's likely that it is the Rhine because the aeroplane is part of the fleet of aircraft owned by Lufthansa, and Lufthansa is German, so it would be fitting if the scene on the cover of the airline magazine was a German scene, *an idyllic green picture, an idyllic Aryan picture, Deutschland, Deutschland über alles.*[10] On the bank of

---

10. *Über alles in der Welt, Wenn es stets zu Schutz und Trutze Brüderlich zusammenhält. Von der Maas bis an die Memel, Von der Etsch bis an den Belt Deutschland, Deutschland über alles, Über alles in der Welt!* Germany, Germany above everything, Above everything in the world, When for protection and defence, it always takes a brotherly stand together. From the Meuse to the Memel, From the Adige to the Belt, Germany, Germany above everything, Above everything in the world! *Deutsche Frauen, deutsche Treue, Deutscher Wein und deutscher Sang Sollen in der Welt behalten Ihren alten schönen Klang, Uns zu edler Tat begeistern Unser ganzes Leben lang. Deutsche Frauen, deutsche Treue, Deutscher Wein und deutscher Sang!* German women,

the river are castles, the one that is in the foreground is smaller than the one in the background but because it is closer it appears to be more grandiose, *how a castle looks from the two-dimensional cover, who is in the window, who looks at me from that closed-in space,* Volker looks at the two-dimensional picture. The castle is large, two people stand in front of it, they are both dressed in uniform, black and green with red epaulettes. The red epaulettes appear as a small dot on each shoulder, there are four red dots in all. The people are small in comparison to the castle, but the epaulettes are visible, soldiers, the two people must be soldiers for they are in uniform, epaulettes on a uniform designate rank, *I suppose if there is no war today there will be one tomorrow, we must make a war, we must imagine how it feels to kill, how it feels to be a hero, a victim, a traitor, the traitor is always sexier than the one he betrays, Judas or Jesus, take your pick, but who is the victor, the betrayer or the betrayed, Judas or Jesus, we must be prepared for all eventualities.* Epaulettes, those pieces of material are a decorative emblem of power, if they were not there the uniform would be just grey-green material covering a body, but a uniform, a uniform of honour, *dishonour,* must be powerfully decorated. The soldiers guard the castles that are behind them, *the Treaty of Versailles, who is the victor now, they will always forgive us, we can act as we please for they*

German loyalty, German wine and German song Shall retain in the world Their old beautiful chime, And inspire us to noble deeds During all of our life. German women, German loyalty, German wine and German song! *Einigkeit und Recht und Freiheit Für das deutsche Vaterland! Danach lasst uns alle streben Brüderlich mit Herz und Hand! Einigkeit und Recht und Freiheit Sind des Glückes Unterpfand; Blüh' im Glanze dieses Glückes, Blühe, deutsches Vaterland!* Unity and justice and freedom For the German Fatherland! For these let us all strive Brotherly with heart and hand! Unity and justice and freedom, Are the pledge of fortune; Flourish in this fortune's glory, Flourish, German Fatherland!

The lyrics are by August Heinrich Hoffmann von Fallersleben and music by Joseph Haydn.

always do, they will always forgive if we say we are sorry, it makes them bigger, life size, who is bigger than me, bigger than those that will never remain small, never remain the velveteen rabbit for you must be real to forgive. Both of the soldiers hold grey rifles, each one has a bayonet on its end, *I want to taste the blood of this annoying air hostess who won't bring me the wine that I ask for, bring me wine, bring me something that will distract me from this eternal flight, bring me something for my senses are deranged, take off your clothes for I am unable to read.* One of the soldiers leans on his rifle, it points downwards into the ground, the other soldier holds his gun at the ready, ready for what may happen on the next page. Volker looks at the picture more closely, behind the soldiers, but just in front of the further castle is a woman, she holds a musical instrument, a gold harp. Volker watches her fingers move over the strings, *I remember the last time we met, the string quartet played Brahms.* He holds the picture to the light, in the corner there is a baby lying on the green ground, he holds the magazine closer to his face, a rabbit peers out from the face of the baby, *a rabbit, not a velveteen rabbit but a real rabbit, real, real, real, the rabbit ascends in whorls of pain, the baby is unhappy, but is the rabbit real, does he even want to be real,* there is no brown on this ground, it is photographically green, greener than fertility, greener than bile. Volker turns the pages of the magazine, he stops turning them only to look at pictures of the bottles of perfume, these are in the last few pages of the magazine. $567.00 –Thierry Mugler: A*MEN PURE COFFEE, FOR THE SELECT FEW.[11] Volker holds the page to his nose, *a hint*

---

11. Thierry Mugler is a master craftsman of fine fashion and fine aroma. He is an artist. He is the creator of the iconic Angel bottle, a faceted star. A*Men Pure Coffee is his new fragrance, the fragrance of fresh coffee beans. Here the top notes open with a deep, roasted coffee bean, which segues to dark chocolate unity. Then, slowly, the middle notes appear, the chocolate melts to become a honeyed liquid coffee, and then come the

*of coffee, tobacco, chocolate, the smell of decadence, a rotten
palimpsest.* Volker coughs, *a forgotten memory, the perfume of
glory days that lingers, the interruption of the accepted banality
of everyday life, the picture makes me want to smoke, Romeo
and Juliet, where is Romeo and the Juliet air hostess who is not
fit for a stage, who is narrating this verbiage, this dirty pleo-
nasm, there is no difference between my life and the narrative of
my life, both are a performance, if I hold a pencil to my lips and
inhale will I feel the smoke course down my throat, touch the
tar with my tongue, taste its pre-worn coat on my lungs.* The
hole on the armrest of the seat that he sits in seems to grow.
The air hostess walks down the aisle; she pushes the drinks
cart, *tart with a cart, trolley dolly,* as she walks past him she
glances down at the magazine. *I want a fly boy, a sailor boy,
the body of the man in the Gaultier[12] perfume poster, the sailor
boy in the striped T-shirt, naked chest, blue stripes, naked chest,
blue stripes, naked chest, blue stripes.* Volker looks out of the
window, it is raining, and nothing is visible except the drops
of water on the window. The double-glazed windows are
made of hardened plastic, *outside I walk through the rain with
my head down,* inside the aeroplane it is dry, the rain cannot
penetrate the hardened plastic, air blows from the air-conditioning pipe above him, *I am always hot, even in the rain I am
hot, the water can never cool me, I must perform in the heat,
the neon lights, the stage lights, the lights on the set, perform as
the director will have me perform, I am a performer, life is a
performance but who is the director, my director, I walk through
the rain with my head down.* The aeroplane moves through
the rain, it moves extremely fast and yet it is slow, deceptively
slow. Volker shields his eyes with a hand and looks outside,

---

base notes of mature cedar, musk and vetiver. Perfume is sensual, it can
disguise.

12. Jean Paul Gaultier is also a master craftsman of fine fashion and fine
aroma. He is known as the artist who dresses Madonna.

the sun is not shining but there is a harsh brilliance, a twinkling reflection, *a diamond as big as, as big as the Dome of the Rock, The Ritz, the rock of crack, glitter, Gary make me glitter*. In the window there is an image of himself, it stares at him, he watches the eyes blink, he licks his lips for they are dry, *Gary make me glitter as if I was a young man*. Outside there is rain and inside Volker shades his eyes, *I am unable to see what it is that is outside, outside there is nothing but the rain*. Volker waits, then he sleeps, then he waits again. The air hostess makes an announcement, it is deracinated, the voice has no foundation, it descends from the loudspeakers, *the aeroplane will be landing shortly, please fasten your seat-belts*. Volker hears *extinguish all cigarettes*, he has forgotten that smoking is no longer permitted on the aeroplane, not even in the toilets, it is a crime to smoke in the sky. The air hostess with the uniform that is fastened tightly across her breasts has a bird-like motif on the front of her dress, *I believe I can fly, I believe I can touch the sky, I am a whore, I am a whore, I am a blue crane, only whores can dance in the sky*, moves down the middle aisle of the C-class section, each time she stops at a seat she looks down at the groin of whoever it is that is sitting there. Often she reaches down to adjust a seat-belt, brushing her hand against whatever groin it is that is there, it is the men who need their seat-belts adjusted, and the occasional woman, *do I want to touch a cunt?* She reaches Volker and looks down at his groin, he feels it move, slightly, imperceptible, *cock sucker*, no one knows this but him, *they all jerk off in the toilets*, nothing is visible, *a stain on my face, a stain on the seat of the toilet, caught*, fasten your seat-belt, we will be landing in ten minutes, the blue bird encircled by the blue circle flutters its wings as her breasts move up and down with each indrawn and exhaled breath, *tit licker*. Volker turns to the window, there is a runway, or rather four runways ahead of him, they are moving closer, the aeroplane will shortly land on one of them. It is twilight and raining, the sun casts an orange glow on the earth, *sepia, photoshop this picture.* The aeroplane banks to the left, the passengers shift slightly towards the left but, as Volker looks around him it appears as if no one but he is aware of this shift. The man in the white T-shirt with the words Princeton Alumni on it looks up from his book, a different book now, Global Economies, the Harvard Guide to Cracking the Code, it is an insignificant shift, not palpable, he can feel it because he is aware of the metal hardness of the seat that is pressed into his left side, there is a metal strut in the arm of the seat that has come loose, it has not broken through the material, yet, but he can feel it press into his rib-cage as the movement of the aeroplane shifts him ever so slightly. *The trolley dolly yaws.* He can make out the perpendicular and parallel runways in the semi-light and the rain, they are wide, as wide as the autobahn that runs from city to city in Germany. The aeroplane comes down closer to the ground, there are numbers on either end of the tar, soon the aeroplane is close enough to the ground to allow him to see the numbers clearly, 09 and 27, these are directions, the numbers of a compass, at the end of the runway that is perpendicular to the one that the aeroplane will land on are lights. As the aeroplane descends several cameras pan[13] across the sky, across the body of the aeroplane, across his body, canvas covers equipment to prevent it from getting wet. Volker moves his face closer to the window, *closeness, the illusion of a close scene, closed in the dark where there is only the light of the camera, the runway is closer,* and it

---

13. A film of the Irish band U2 performing Beautiful Day was made on a runway at Charles de Gaulle airport. In the video Jumbo jets take off and land. The heart is a bloom, etc, etc … Should you want to read more of the lyrics of this song log in to Wikipedia or any other website that gives the lyrics of songs. Unfortunately, these lyrics cannot be reproduced here as U2 own the copyright; they own these words. Legal action may be taken if they are quoted without permission.

is closer, imperceptibly so. *Where am I going, what will I do when I get there, what, where, what?*

AND THAT WAS then, now Volker follows the line of people, they do not form a straight line, it is a quavering line of walking figures, some tall, some short, some with hair and some without, *silver hair, it reminds me of her, the copulations that will never be again, I am waking the dead from sleep that is not sleep, will the dead arise from a grave, a garden grave, she looks like Mary Magdalene, Jesus fucked Mary Magdalene up the arse.* Some people follow directly behind the person in front of them, others walk slightly to the side, there are few colours in the line, most of the people are dressed in grey, *not grey-silver, not silver-grey. I am running away from imagination, whose imagination, my imagination, oh Eurydice, why were you taken to the underworld, why were you bitten by the snake, I was bitten by the snake, I cannot play the lyre, shall I ever find you, I will find you and then I will look back and we will be lost.* Volker keeps to the centre of the line …

AT THE ENTRANCE to the Business Class lounge stands a man. He is very tall and wears a white T-shirt. On the front is written 'I Love Dick' in black, and on the back it says 'Chris Kraus is sexy'.[14] He is Dick, some might say the

14. Chris Kraus, a 39-year-old experimental film maker, and Sylvère Lotringer, a 56-year-old college professor from New York, have dinner with Dick ____, an acquaintance of Sylvère's, at a sushi bar in Pasadena. (Dick is later outed as Dick Hebdige, an Australian cultural critic who has recently moved to LA.) Over dinner the two men discuss recent trends in postmodern critical theory and Chris, who is no intellectual, notices Dick making continual eye contact with her … This is the start of Chris Kraus's scandalous and cult feminist novel *I Love Dick*. Kraus is especially good on sexual shame and self-abasement, the intolerable torment when you offer yourself and aren't wanted; or, as Kraus says 'shame is what you feel after being fucked on quaaludes by some art world cohort who'll pretend it never happened, shame is what you feel after giving blow jobs in the

words on his T-shirt indicate a case of extreme narcissism, a famous (to a few people), and semi-famous (to fewer), and unknown (to many) creator of performance art. He holds his glass of what appears to be tequila to his red lips and smiles at anyone who catches his pale blue eyes for he likes to talk about his lesser known craft, his unknown genius. Claudine, tired, sits; or rather she lies back, on a settee in the Business Class lounge. She hates it when Dick is here, she does not catch his eyes, he is always shamefully loud, and all she wants to do is rest. She is just glad that today he is alone, without his cohort of acolytes who seem to fol-low him wherever he goes. She has planned to meet Jim/ Peter here, and maybe Thierry, if he can escape the crowds who wish to spray fragrances on their arms and necks, but neither of them is here yet. Claudine wonders if she forgot to send them the text message with this plan, or if she forgot to put the correct time in the message, but then thinks that if she did not remember and they do not come to the lounge because she gave them the wrong time, she is tired and would rather have a vodka alone anyway.

Jean Claude, whom Claudine does not know but could swear she has seen in the lounge before, is also in the busi-ness class lounge. He is not allowed to be in here, but has stolen in, invisibly, because he wanted a break from work, a break from studying who is rich and who is not, and this can often be difficult and tiresome, which is why Claudine may or may not have seen him. He loiters – some may say suspi-ciously – close to the long beds that line the walls at the back, the beds where those who really wish to sleep, or to have semi-private semi-public sex, can do so undisturbed. Clau-dine, if she has seen him here, he might be familiar because he is in the airport often, thinks that he is a thief, a pretty

---

bathroom at Max's Kansas City because Liza Martin wants free coke.' But shame, says Kraus, is how a powerless woman can take back her power, for shame is a role, and so it can be played.

thief, but can't be sure as he has never tried to steal anything from her. Why would he, she has nothing to steal.

On one of the beds, right at the back of the lounge, possibly to be further out of the way of prying voyeuristic eyes – it seems to have been there a long time because, incongruously for this lounge, the metal sides are slightly rusted, the mattress is sagging, and pieces of cloth and wire protrude from where the sheets are torn – is a woman. Her hair is black, not dead-bird black like a raven, but black with gleams of silver. She lies on the bed and does not move, it is possible that she is dead, as her throat has been torn almost in half and her wide-open thighs are covered in blood. She could be, if one did not know different, an art work placed there for discerning Business Class travellers to look at and wonder what the world of art is coming to what with all these violent images.

Claudine does not see this very real art work, is it art, a performance, because she is tired and so her eyes are closed. Instead she dreams that before her, in a smart room with an incongruous dilapidated bed, is a dying body. Claudine does not know that this dream is real, she is wide awake, she just pretends to dream because the reality is too ghastly. Jean Claude, who Claudine does not see, watches the injured woman as she raises her hands to her throat; the fingers of her right hand try to close the wound while her left hand rests on the wide open slit on her thigh, she is trying to stop the blood for it must be stopped if she is to live.

The man wearing the T-shirt with I Love Dick written on it does not watch the dying woman, instead he watches the television screen that hangs above the reception desk which has no attendants at it, about three metres away from the line of couch beds, a boy band mimes the words of a song, German words. He cannot speak German. Neither can Jean Claude. So both do not know that it is a parody of the German national anthem lip-synced by a famous anarchist rock group, and that they also sing, or lip-sing, those words that have, since the

Nazi regime was defeated, been banned in Germany. The boys are blond, they prance on the screen, actors on an international stage, but what does Jean Claude care for the words of the song, the meaning of these words, all he knows is that the music seems particularly apt to the scene he is witnessing. It is military and arrogant and violent.

The woman is mortally wounded; she moves slackly, she wheezes almost inaudibly, maybe for the last time. She looks at him and tries to call out, but Jean Claude knows that he is almost invisible where he's crouching behind another of the couch beds, she cannot be calling to him. He is not a passenger, he merely works in the airport terminal, sometimes, and so he hides; and anyway he cannot hear her because the boy band voices swell the airwaves, the sound dances a ballerina dance, the boys pirouette on one leg, the image embraces the woman.

The dying woman looks at Claudine, but she is asleep, her head has fallen backwards and her mouth is slightly open, from it emerges a faint purr, as if she is a cat. She is dressed in a black, red and gold dress, the material is made of horizontal stripes; the colours are lurid, bold, more striking than they would be on a flag held aloft at a rally, or hanging on a pole outside a court-house, or drooped, shrinking at half-mast on the day that Hitler died. The gold tries to cover her legs. It is a short dress, it is smeared with red, it is her blood that seeps from the wound between her legs. The red stripe, a little higher, a band across her stomach, is possibly redder than it would ordinarily be for it is also coated in her blood. There is blood spatter on the floor beside her. And the black stripe? Jean Claude does not notice if it, too, is covered in blood as it is a colour on which red is not easily seen. He crouches down, his head between his legs, and wonders who tortured this woman. Who was the victor that plundered her body? He breathes deeply for he is afraid.

Claudine also breathes deeply. In her dream she sees a woman who was on the aeroplane on which she finished her shift two hours ago. With the woman was a child, a particularly irksome child who he did not sit still, this insignificant woman with red hair, in Claudine's dream, the woman carries in her left hand a sharp knife that appears to have been taken from the buffet table and in her right a broken glass.

THE LINE TREMBLES, *if I fall out of line I will lose track, the track, I must go somewhere far away, far away, the line will lead to somewhere, did I love her only because she was incapable of understanding me, if she understood me she could never have inspired me, my love is a misunderstanding, I love you only as you are, a limitation, you will never understand, this is the reason you arouse me, this is your vitality and my illusion.* From the intercom system, in three languages, French, English and German, comes an announcement. Expect many delays as there is an ongoing strike by the airport's baggage handlers. The airport management apologises for any inconvenience. Passengers must collect all luggage from the baggage carousel, it will not be forwarded to the final destination. Sniffer dogs will be in the area so as to ensure that passengers need not clear customs should they be in transit. Volker follows the line of people as he listens to the announcement, which is almost immediately followed by another announcement, Will[15] the

---

15. The passenger in question is Will Self, who is going to miss his flight to another country, where he is supposed to talk about why he is sometimes referred to as a lyric poet of the metropolis, because he has left his boarding pass on a bookshelf in the airport curio shop and feels disinclined to return and collect it. He is Baudelairean, the ultimate hero of modernity, a figure who gives voice to paradox and illusion, who participates in, while being the outsider. The bad boy, he thinks outside the boundaries laid down by the society in which he lives; he writes about sex, drugs and violence. Will Self is a class warrior storming the citadels of the literary establishment. And yet, as an Oxford-educated, middle-class metropolitan who, despite his protestations to the contrary, is the heart of the establishment. He says that he does not write fiction for people to identify with; he does not create a picture of a world they can recognise. He writes to astonish people. What excites him is to disturb a reader's fundamental

passenger delaying Flight … but he can't hear which flight or the name of the passenger for this information is obscured by an unpleasant crackle of static. For an instant he stops walking and frowns as he anticipates the delay, *where am I going to, where are we going to, we are going forward, forward is good, what is evil if only the absence of good, we are going backwards, why do I need to hurry there is nowhere to go to,* he feels someone bump into him from behind. He looks up at a woman with red hair, he does not fall he simply staggers forward, an almost fall, he looks behind him in an attempt to locate the woman who struck him but she has already moved on, or if she has not and is still behind him, *does she want to harm me, how can I stave off this chaos, there is no order,* she gives no indication that she may have touched him, there is nothing personal, tangible, *touch, the human touch, I want to stab you, hit you, hurt you, because I crave the human touch, harm me, harm me, make me feel pain, glorify your world by causing me pain, impose your laws on me and so cause me pain, cut my veins for then you will feel my blood,* he steadies himself quickly for the painted line of people moves fast, faster, for all the people in the line have a destination, they are going somewhere, they have a purpose, *all people must have a purpose, we must all have a purpose, I am an ant, a worker ant, a busy bee, a worker bee that cares for the silver queen, would die for the queen, I am an ant, I am a small man, I know the mobility of your soul, your immobile soul that inspires for it does not understand, my story is your story, the same story can be told by anyone, everyone.* A woman with bright red hair, the same woman who may have bumped into him earlier, he cannot be sure, *they all look the same, nondescript, we all have red hair, underneath*

---

assumptions. He also says that the literary novel as an art work is dying, that there is an active resistance to difficulty in all its aesthetic manifestations, and this is accompanied by a sense of dull pulsating grievance which conflates thinking with elitism.

it is brown, it is never red, never brown, red-brown, always pale, and who wears a pair of dark loose-fitting trousers, *unflattering, self-contained vanity,* hurries past him, *again,* but this time she is hurrying in another direction, *the world is always in a hurry, it is tiring.* She holds the hand of a child, the child has blue eyes and red-blonde hair, *her hair is a real red, a real colour, an ideological uprising, the ersatz rabbit is really real,* a man child, the child does not want to move fast, the woman drags him in her wake and he is heavy, the pale beige skin of her face is covered in patches of red, *red hair, red cheeks, red skin,* she must use a lot of energy dragging the child who does not want to hurry, and she must hurry for she has somewhere to go, *nowhere ...*

HELGA IS RUNNING as if she is running from something, but she has nowhere to go. Neither does Gunther, the child she drags behind her. She stops abruptly, almost crashing into the man who is walking in front of her, but then she begins to run again. She runs because she has done something hideous, she wants to hide, even she is unable to believe that she could do such a thing. She thinks she can now hide in the open, just sit in a chair in the terminal and wait, wait for the announcement of the aeroplane that she will catch, the return flight to Frankfurt.

It all began a long time ago when Helga discovered that her husband was having sex with another woman, a sexually tumultuous affair. And so she searched for and found this woman. Kurt is Helga's husband. They live in Frankfurt. Helga does not know the name of the woman her husband has sex with; the only thing she knows is that Kurt is not having sex with her, so he must be having sex with someone else. Kurt was always curt with Helga, always brusque, although he never beat her, he has never even laid a hand on her, not violently, nor sexually for a while, but he was not very friendly. And he had given up on her body for once she had the child,

Gunther, a boy, Kurt's genetic line was secure. His name would continue.

Kurt Braun, Braun, a name that is not uncommon. Kurt is insignificant, ordinary, indistinguishable from all other men of his thirty-something age and ethnicity, he is not even related to Eva Braun, now that would have been something to distinguish him from others, the other Brauns who lived in the same street, in the same suburb, in the same city, this was something he could have boasted about. Unfortunately, he is just simply a Braun, one of many, and his Nazi lineage is not illustrious. He did have Nazis in his family; his father was a part of the Hitler Youth and his grandfather a guard in Auschwitz, but they were just ordinary Nazis. They did not know Hitler personally, they did not share his bed or his bunker with him when he died.

Kurt has no politics; he upholds what meta systems there are and feels no shame for his nation's past. Kurt is instinctive rather than intellectual, he is not a thinker. He chose a lissome girl ten years younger than himself so as to breed, for although he is insignificant and meagre he knows that breeding is in his blood, he has to breed. Unfortunately, in the Christian society he lives in, he had to marry this girl, his breeding machine, for only by marriage would his offspring bear his name, the memorable name of Braun. And so from Helga, Gunther was born, Gunther Braun. Then Kurt set out to find another, someone he could have sex with, and he did. He found someone else.

She works in a haberdashery[16] and her name is Marie.

---

16. A haberdashery is a store that sells cloth, pins, thread, pincushions, and any other items necessary for sewing. Haberdasheries still exist in Germany, although they are becoming fewer and fewer as time passes. In most other countries the haberdashery, like the café, has been incorporated into large department stores that are owned by large corporations that brook no competition and so try, at all costs, to squeeze out the little man, or woman, or, in this case, the little haberdashery.

Marie is blonde, her hair was a light colour rather than golden. However, she was able, due to modern chemicals, to make it golden, but she did genuinely have light hair. Kurt knew this because her pubic hair was light, a sure sign, that is, when she did not shave it off, for he enjoyed the childlike appeal of a hairless pubis. He had, prior to embarking upon this clandestine affair, looked at a lot of pornography and in it the women with shaven pubes were the most appealing. And so he told this to Marie and she obligingly shaved her cunt for him.

Helga and Gunther live with Kurt in a small suburb somewhere in Frankfurt, small, not that small, but small as all suburbs are small; a big city is, after all, made of many small suburbs. Helga takes care of Gunther, and the house and the shopping and Kurt. And Kurt goes off to work every day. He works as a machine operator in a factory that makes brake parts for smart cars. Their list of clients is large – Mercedes-Benz, Volkswagen, even some foreign companies. Peugeot. The French need good brakes, otherwise their cars would slide into other cars and Europe would be a mess of broken down cars (like America). He also goes off every evening to Marie; sometimes he does not even return home. Marie has no illusions as to the future of this relationship, or so Kurt likes to think, but actually she does. This is a cliché, the ever wanting and waiting woman, but most clichés are correct (they wouldn't be clichés otherwise). Marie really does hope that Kurt will leave Helga and come and live with her. He will bring Gunther with him, they could be a real family, and then she would not need to shave her cunt and drink and laugh with him and, most of all, she would never have to apologise to him again. Never is a strong word, women always apologise to men and will continue to do so, but possibly Marie could do it less frequently.

Helga knows about this affair, Kurt never hid it. But Helga longs for Kurt and a real family and, unfortunately, Marie also longs for Kurt and a real family. This stalemate changed abruptly one day when a man walked into the haberdashery. He was tall, whereas Kurt was short, he was dark whereas Kurt was blond, he was bourgeois, in the upper regions, whereas Kurt was working class, in the upper regions. Marie knew which side her bread was buttered on and so when the man proposed that they go for lunch and then a supper and then somewhere where there was a bed to lie on Marie dropped Kurt like a stone. And Marie now waxed her cunt, she did not shave it. And when the man said Hey let's go to Vienna for a weekend, Flight Centre Frankfurt Travel has a special on, a Business Class Lufthansa flight to Paris, and then an Economy Class ticket on to Vienna, with no stopping at customs for this is the European Union and what is the union for but this convenience, and, although the waiting time between flights may be long, it can be spent in the opulent and sumptuous Business Class lounge of the International Departures terminal, Marie had packed her bags.

HELGA DID NOT know that the woman with whom Kurt was having sex with was no longer having sex with him because Kurt still spent his evenings out. Now, instead of fucking Marie, he drank, for he could not believe that Marie had left him for another, and neither could he believe that he was stuck with Helga. And so he drank and imagined that he was tall and dark and that he had a harem of nymphs who gave him succour when it was required. And Helga, who had read many detective novels, and who used to as a result of this knowledge go frequently to the haberdashery in order to conduct surveillance overheard Marie telling someone on the telephone about her weekend trip to Vienna via Paris with a man, possibly Kurt, or a brother or cousin or just a friend, but most definitely a man, and so she cashed in her savings and, together with Gunther, he had to go with her for who would take care of him while she was away for the day, boarded an aeroplane to Paris, the same aeroplane that Marie travelled on, the same aeroplane on which Claudine worked. Helga sat close to Marie and the man who was not Kurt (but then Kurt might be on another flight) or her brother or just her friend and wondered why they seemed so intimate, so loving, as Helga knew that Marie was having an affair with Kurt and this, if it is what Helga thought, was a betrayal, and even though Kurt was already betraying her, she could feel his hurt and pain should he find out that Marie was betraying him. She thought the man may have been a bit slow, slow in the head, for Helga noticed that he talked all the time and she knew that people who were slow talked a lot, a lot of nonsense. She did not like to think this of Kurt, but she often felt it.

Gunther loved the aeroplane, he had never flown before, and, as he was unaware of what his mother intended, he ran up and down the aisle, much to the chagrin of the other passengers and Claudine, who just wanted an hour or so of peace and quiet and no distractions.

Marie was difficult to follow once the aeroplane was on the ground for Helga knew her to be blonde, a golden bottle blonde, what a slut, but now she was black, her hair was like a raven's, the raven that sat on the telephone post at the end of the street in which she and Kurt lived. Helga thought that black hair was horrible as ravens are malevolent and vicious and evil, and Germans are blonde and kind and good. Marie and the man, her brother or her cousin or her friend, as Helga believed, walked past the luggage carousel and into what looked like a prestigious lounge. They had one bag, Helga recognised it for Kurt had given her the same one, a large one with a Louis Vuitton emblem. Marie was given the bag by Kurt when they were still fucking, it was a fake, he had picked it up in a flea market in Frankfurt, from a Chinaman. The lounge was not one for just the ordinary person, and Helga was ordinary, but she raised up her head as if she belonged there, bravery comes with a fervent belief, and followed them inside anyway. Then she hid behind a sofa bed. Gunther was instructed by Helga to be cute and quiet and to sit on a chair at the entrance of the lounge and as he, in this instance, did as he was told, he went unnoticed for small children in prestigious lounges, if they are quiet, are never noticed, they just happen to be there, they may be waiting for a nanny or a mother in the massage parlour, this was free for passengers who were able to go into this lounge. Children are just part of the scenery.

Marie and her brother or her cousin or her friend found a place to sit on a bed that was in a darker recess of the lounge, they wanted to be private, and the man, much to Helga's horror, wanted a blow job. Then the man went into the bathroom, he was able to manage alone, despite being drunk, he could not walk straight or upright, but he managed. He was there a long time. Helga got up and looked into the bathroom, even though it was a men's bathroom. He had passed out, he was lying on the floor. She then walked confidently to the buffet table and, while looking as if she was deciding on something sweet or savoury, surreptitiously picked up a long steel steak knife and a crystal champagne glass. Now she was ready to move in for the kill. First she distracted Marie, she asked Gunther to run past her and fall onto the floor crying, then while Marie was helping Gunther to get up, and consoling him and wiping away the tears that Helga had instructed him to cry, Helga put some powder in Marie's vodka cocktail. Marie did not notice this for, besides helping Gunther, she was also drunk and getting drunker as she drank those entitled extras that were included in this special offer. Helga had bought the powder from the chemist who had a shop down the road from where she lived, fast-acting sleeping powder. When the chemist asked her why she needed such a strong sleeping tablet she replied that it was for her ancient mother who, because she was in extreme pain, suffered from insomnia. Helga dropped a large amount of the powder into Marie's vodka. In no time at all Marie was quiet, her head drooped down and soon she was making the small sounds of sleep.

Helga then took the opportunity, as there was no one in the lounge, no one awake, that is – the air hostess who had been attending to all her needs on the flight to Paris was asleep in a far corner of the lounge and, Helga did not think, could see her even if she woke, the man at the doorway in the T-shirt that said I Love Dick had moved out of the lounge, he was still there, Helga could hear his voice, but he was far away and anyway he was engrossed in himself, and she could not see Jean Claude hiding behind the bed that was next to the one that Marie was on – to stab Marie at least twenty times with the steak knife and then she cut her face and inner thighs with the glass, which she had smashed onto the wall so that it was jagged and sharp, in the most appalling and bloody manner. She wanted Marie to suffer, she didn't want her to die without any pain. Once she had stabbed and savagely cut Marie's body she left the lounge, taking Gunther by the hand as if she had only walked into the wrong place and time.

Helga looks at her watch, 9h30, how fast time goes when something that you enjoy happens, the killing had only taken forty-five minutes, but now she needs to run for she knows that she will need to get far away so as not to be a suspect in this heinous crime. She suspects that the luggage on the carousel will have come and gone by now, and so is relieved that neither she nor Gunther have luggage, what would they need it for as they were only to spend a few hours in this foreign airport.

Sometime later Helga and Gunther caught the next flight back to Frankfurt. And when they returned to Frankfurt it was as if nothing had happened. Kurt continued to work at the brake parts factory and Helga continued to take care of

Gunther and Kurt and the house in the suburbs. And Kurt never knew why he now found her irresistible and sexy, or why Gunther had begun to wet his bed at night.

But this is in the future, not now. Now Helga is moving very fast in the airport, going nowhere. She does not know that Jean Claude witnessed this murderous act, but even so, this is of no consequence as Jean Claude will not say a word to anyone. After all, he is not allowed to be in the Business Class lounge for he is a thief. And Gunther, he knows that blood is very red and has a strange smell, much like the smell that comes from the pan that his sausage is cooked in.

IN THE LOUNGE Claudine wakes from her dream. There, to her right and slightly behind her, is a dead, tortured girl. And so Claudine thinks that she will stay in the lounge, for what could be better for her than to be a witness in a bloody killing. The airline cannot fire her until the murder is cleared up, and she will be a celebrity, a celebrity in the small world of the airlines.

No, no one is any the worse off, except Marie, and possibly Gunther, who will never forget the sight and smell of blood. In later years he will become a militant vegetarian and campaign actively for the end of the meat trade.

VOLKER HAS NO choice, he must move fast because everyone is moving fast, *there is a delay, there is no hurry, am I always delayed, do I come too late, too late to hold her, too late to love her,* he must hurry, the line of people moves faster and then it stops and should he not move he will fall too because the crowd will sweep him along. Then abruptly he stops, he looks around him, the moving line is now a stationary line, only occasionally does it move, a hand leans out to hold a trolley, there is the shrug of a shoulder so that the bag held there becomes more comfortable, there are voices around him, voices that emanate from the mouths of those that are in the line, *blah blah, talking heads, we're on the road to nowhere, where is the secret, the silent secret,* voices from the microphones in the ceiling, voices that tell him where to go and what he should do, *where can I hide,* where he can drink or eat, where, should he desire, he can have a massage or go to the toilet. A young man or is it a boy, stands to his right, the boy man, a man boy, moves closer to him. Volker looks at the boy man and smiles, as he smiles he hears a voice, a microphone voice, be aware, be alert, a stranger may offer you sweets, do not take them, hold your bags carefully there are pickpockets around every corner. Volker continues to look at the boy man, *why would I want this boy, this man boy, when I have a memory of her silver hair, do I struggle against this power, the power that she has, is this my struggle, the struggle of memory against forgetting, do I want to forget for if I do my divine right will be eclipsed, I will rule no longer.*

To Volker's left, close to the entrance of the Business Class lounge and next to a tall man in a white T-shirt with the words 'Chris Kraus is sexy' written on the back of it, is a stationary man, a breathing statue, a statement. The tall man moves towards this statue and moves one of its arms, and then the lips into a grimace. The statue's fleshy face is covered in blue paint on which are white stars, the body is painted with red and white lines, at his feet is a bowl, it has several burned dollar bills in it, *money burning, the flames are not real but there is, there is, an American conflagration,* in his hands is a sign that says 'whither goest thou, America, in thy shiny car in the night',[17] *Americans are everywhere, dying rotting skeletons cars ...*

---

17. Jack Kerouac wrote *On the Road,* the story of a road trip across America. Jack Kerouac was slim and blond and heterosexual; the all-American good-looking boy who could, sometimes, be a rebel, he was often referred to as the James Dean of the book. Truman Capote was also blond, but he was short and fat and homosexual and sometimes a bitch. Capote said that *On the Road* was not writing but typing.

JEAN CLAUDE is nineteen years old. He is a thief, the always to be found in an airport, or any other crowded space, pickpocket. He works for, or is employed by, a pickpocket group; some would call it a loose group of thieves, others a gang, but these terms connote something inchoate, unstructured, disorganised. In fact it is a well-organised formal organisation, in other circumstances, and should it be socially acceptable, it could have been a registered financial services company, or a hedge fund, or even a bank. The organisation is not merely a group of people; it is a corporation, with branches in all the major cities of France. The Paris group, or subsidiary, is the largest division in the corporation. They work in all the airports, stations and bus stations of the city. In each transport hub at least two, sometimes three, pickpockets work.

The group, or gang, has a hierarchy, a corporate hierarchy. There is a central structure in which there is a chairman and board of directors, they manage the entire organisation. Each division, the Paris division is no different, has a management structure and many workers. There is a divisional chairman. In Paris he is charismatic, cruel, dogmatic and educated. He always uses Voltaire's words, Man is born free but is everywhere in chains, to motivate the pickpockets. They are, he explains enchained by what is defined as right, and he, or the organisation, can give them the opportunity to be free, to earn money, to determine their own destiny. Who cares what is right or wrong anyway? What he does not say is that the freedom he believes in is his own, not that of others. He earns a lot of money from his pickpocket workers. He is often compared to Steve Jobs because another of his much-repeated phrases is 'An apple a day keeps the cops away'. And the chairman eats nothing but fruit, he is a fruitarian, and he loves apples, the ripe red ones. He does not believe in killing, either another human being or animals, and so he does not encourage the use of violence among his workers.

Then there is a training officer who determines what

training is required to be a successful pickpocket. To be a pickpocket is not merely to be a thief. It is a skill and requires many hours of training; how to distract a person without them being aware that this is a distraction, how to reach into a pocket without the other feeling anything, and most of all how to identify the most lucrative target and, once identified, in which pocket or bag the most valuable items are. In this group the chairman insists that all pickpockets, no matter what they say their previous experience is, must be trained from inception. As it is, most of the recruits know little or nothing at all about pickpocketing so the training officer is always busy devising new courses, assessing who needs further training or empowerment, and, of course, whether or not a person can, in fact, come up to scratch, or if he is un-trainable.

There is also the financial officer, who determines what each pickpocket is paid. A pickpocket does not steal and then keep the proceeds of his efforts; all stolen goods are centralised and then either sold immediately, or kept for a period and then sold. If the goods are of no value at all, rather than return whatever it is to the lost property department of the particular transport hub from where it came, they are destroyed. There are harsh penalties for keeping things stolen to oneself. Often a wallet is taken; travellers often imagine that wherever it is they are going will have no cash available. This is especially true in the airports, and if they are American or European and are going into Africa for the first time, they do not know and cannot imagine that an African city has auto tellers in it. Africa is backward and wild; tigers walk in the streets of the cities there.[18] And jewellery. Women frequently put

18. In fact there are no tigers in Africa, except in 2000, when the South African film maker and landowner John Varty brought several tigers to his farm in Philippolis, in the Free State, in order to start the first tiger breeding programme outside Asia. Varty made two films, *Living with Tigers* and *Tiger Man of Africa*, which have been criticised by environmentalists as being

their valuable jewellery into the pockets of their jackets or dresses. They imagine to wear it is too dangerous, it may be stolen, or it may be detected by a wary customs official, and so they hide it. They are unaware that it is better to wear jewellery, it is less easy to steal and most customs officials cannot tell a diamond from diamanté.

Then of course there is the human resources officer. He is the one who finds the new recruits, interviews them, identifies who has potential or experience or the desired qualifications. Qualifications are particularly important. A good pickpocket is also a semiotician: he can read the signs and can quote Barthes to any unsuspecting traveller. But there is a nasty side to this position of human resources officer. Part of the job is to manage the number of pickpockets, and sometimes it is necessary to let a pickpocket go, he could be retrenched, in which case a package is paid to his loved ones, his elderly mother or his fiancée or child, and then he is relocated deep down under; or he could be dismissed for some kind of misconduct, thrown into the Seine with rocks in his pockets and his throat slit from ear to ear.

Jean Claude is nineteen but he looks much younger, he could be mistaken for fourteen. His face is smooth, hardly a hair on it, his eyes are black and he has extremely long eyelashes. He is regularly teased by the other employees for being girlish, a pansy. His skin is dark, not black, for although he is of African extraction – his grandfather, on his mother's side, was born in Senegal and his grandmother, on his father's side, was Algerian – this colour has been so whitened out in his breeding that now he is merely coffee. He wishes he was darker, to be black is sexy, or so he thinks. He listens to a lot of American rap music and loves Snoop Dogg,

---

only made to boost Varty's fading and faltering ego while taking tigers from their natural habitat. In 2012, as divine justice will have it, Varty was seriously injured by two of his tigers. He has never fully recovered from his injuries.

and of course all Africans are known to have large cocks.

Jean Claude was born in Paris, he has never left the city, he has never caught a train to the provinces or the Mediterranean, he does not know what an ocean looks like, and neither does he know a tree that has not been manicured.

Jean Claude is a distracter, not a pickpocket. His preferred method of distraction is to approach a man, or woman, but most often it is a man, flirt with him, and then when the man is confused, for Jean Claude never flirts with obviously gay men, he pretends to feign indifference, which then gets their attention for no man wants to be rebuffed, or sometimes the man thinks that he is being molested and is afraid, but of course he will never call the police, or any attention to himself, this would be unmanly, and in all these instances, the man is confused and so does not concentrate on his bags or pockets.

Jean Claude is very good at his job. He is one of the highest paid distracters in the organisation. He is going far, climbing the corporate ladder, in the future he aims to become the divisional chairman or at least the financial officer. Prior to this position as a pickpocket – this is his first job – he studied at the Sorbonne, he is not only skilled, but well educated.

The German, who almost walked into the mime with the bowl at his feet, who did not flinch, did not blink, is not well dressed, nor does he look wealthy. Jean Claude supposes he is German because he is dressed for the cold, although it is not cold in the airport but, being a German this is sometimes difficult to detect and – Jean Claude knows this is a gross generalisation but unfortunately it is true – Germans often wear the most unstylish and cheap clothes. Jean Claude walks away, maybe he will go and look for Maria, the older Bulgarian woman he met a few days ago outside the toilets. Yes, he feels like a break from work, and yes, he never did take the lunch break. And he would like to tell Maria about the dying woman he just saw, it was more like a movie than real and Maria, she is in the movie industry.

VOLKER MOVES RELUCTANTLY behind a fat woman who is close to the baggage carousel where he now, unfortunately, due to the strike by the baggage handlers, has to find his suitcase, *nuisances are annoying*, even though he does not have to go through customs with them, she is a voice controlled by a South London accent and a face pulled and stretched back by her scraped back naturally, *unnaturally*, black hair, *the council estate facelift*, blah blah, foin'd the hubbie yet luv, fook him, why is this bloody thing taking so long, fook the frogs, there is no reply from whomever it is she is speaking to, she does not appear concerned to receive a reply, she is speaking to tell the people around her about herself, *tell them how she ate, slept, spent her childhood on the council estate*, she is belligerent, even aggressive, for there is nothing more important than what she wants to say. She turns to look at the boy man, fookin black bastard, they are everywhere these days, where is my bag? Volker does not look at her, *how stupid she is, she has an answer for everything, she can never comprehend anything as a question*, she seizes his arm, *a world of answers, the fearsome nosiness of her certainty. I hate these dogs they sniff eternally, these three black Alsatians, these Nazi dogs, maybe they will bite me, bite her.* The dark boy man has red lips, red lips that Volker wants to kiss, *red lips burn, lips encircle my balls, this is my doomed attempt to revive a cliché, is my life a cliché? I am comfortable with the cliché because I know it so well, will this be an interlude, a fantastic phantom, an interruption, I want to feel a body, the skin of youth*, he moves away, the boy man moves away too. *He's onto me, or is he? Don't think I can do it, don't think I want to, he is watching me so closely, he will follow me, I am stalking him, I am stalking him, I am stalking a lost love, a lost deed, I will do this deed.* The man boy has somewhere to go, someone else to meet, he has a destination. Volker wears a dark red jersey over which he wears a green parka, it was cold in the place that he came from, the boy man is dressed only in a white T-shirt, with the words Calvin Klein written in black emblazoned on the front, and torn blue jeans, his ankles slim and delicate, *Narcissus*[19] *stares into the pool of water, his lips smile*. It is hot inside the building but Volker cannot carry his parka because his hands are full, or rather they will be full when his bag arrives on the carousel that already starts to move. Volker stands at this carousel; he has been standing here for more than an hour, to collect his luggage. He is annoyed, Lufthansa always send a passenger's bags onward to their final destination, but today because of the strike they could not do this. And there is an irritating number of dogs walking around, Alsatians, sniffing all the bags, *better than a queue for customs and the eyes of the enemy boring into me*, some even sniffing at the crotches of the passengers, *the French are poor and lazy, it's no wonder that we could march right into Paris, frog communists, bite them, bite them, make them work harder*, consequently only a skeleton staff, *scabs, solidarity is broken, I am not a betrayer, I will not cross the line, I have only a strand of hair, a line of silver across the pillow*, and the employees working were used to

19. The story of Narcissus, as related by Ovid in the *Metamorphoses*, is a story of self-love and the echo of always longing for another. One day Narcissus was walking in the woods when Echo, a mountain nymph, saw him and fell in love. Echo, obsessed with desire, followed him everywhere. But Narcissus knew that he was being followed and so he cried out 'Who's there?' and Echo called back 'Who's there?' Then she could watch no longer. She wanted him, she needed his touch, the sound of his voice. And so she showed him who she was. She ran up to him and tried to embrace him. But Narcissus was cold. He loved only himself, and so he walked away. Echo was grief-struck; her words were destroyed. She spent the rest of her life speaking only to herself, and always only the echo of another's words. But vengeance was near: Nemesis, the goddess of revenge, learned of this occurrence and she decided to punish Narcissus. She lured him to a pool, where, as he leaned forward and cupped water in his hands, he saw his own reflection. He fell in love with the beautiful boy who was before him. Many years went by as Narcissus tried to woo his love, tried to touch his love, but every time he leaned towards him, every time he spoke, his love would ripple and dissipate and disappear into the water. And so Narcissus committed suicide.

take the bags on and off aeroplanes, not to move them from one aeroplane to another. Now, after this delay, this delay of more than an hour, closer to an hour and a half, circles of luggage move on the carousel, a red suitcase, a yellow backpack, a cardboard box, all of these move past him, *is my life delayed, why am I always too late,* the carousel is not in a hurry although the people around it are, quick grab it, hurry that's mine, shut-up you arsehole, fuck you, Jesus these people are slow, can't they move, move it, get out of the way. And if they do not look at the carousel for their luggage they stare intently at the small screens that they hold in front of their faces, this crowd, they are all squeezed up against each other staring at the blinking screen that they hold in their hands, *fingers punch out an imitation of a life.* Volker looks at a man, he is dressed in shorts and a Hawaiian sunset adorns his vest, a sound emerges from his mouth, a bubble of spittle lands on the front of his vest, *a sound bite*, he shouts, moves quickly, almost at a run to where the conveyor belt begins to move, the mouth of a tunnel, black rubber hanging in front of it, the man snatches at a suitcase, the man reaches forward too late, the bag has eluded him, edged forward on the moving carousel, then the man runs to where the bag has moved to, but there are people standing in front of him. Volker watches his inquietude, his weariness, the Hawaiian sunset of his shirt is wet, *storm clouds of suffering, when will suffering ever be justified, when it is beautiful, the raw material of a beauty, my suffering for her is beautiful, elegiac, this is not beautiful, this man is foul, his reach can never exceed his grasp and a man's reach must exceed his grasp for what is heaven but to reach higher, a higher place above a moving merry-go-round, I reach out, where am I, I have been to heaven, I am in heaven, a simulated heaven, my god is now a life-size doll.* The man does not manage to lift his bag from the conveyor belt, his face is filled with anguish, there are tears in his eyes, *he cannot accept that his luggage will disappear, disappear into an indifferent universe,* he runs further along the line, people curse as he flays the air, his desperation is palpable, it punches the air, *there is the smell of desolation, of perspiration, hopefulness, hope is the most pernicious of all the evils, he hopes for his luggage, he hopes he will not disappear.* The man in the vest with the sweat-stained Hawaiian sunset painted on it takes his bag from the moving space where he began, he has moved, around the carousel, *did he move forward, sad, this is sad, sadder, there are few things that are sadder than the truly monstrous?* Volker stands and watches the different bags, he waits, *I will wait forever for a bag that is inconsequential, I do not need what it contains,* for his own to appear, his black bag that has few clothes in it, underwear, a shirt, a pair of jeans, some toiletries, a razor and toothpaste, and his mouth organ, *underneath the lamppost by the barrack hall*[20] *I will sit alone and wait for you, A minor, E flat, where is my bag, will it appear or is it lost, as I am lost, I am lost without my mouth organ, I want to kiss it, caress it, hold it to my lips; make music, the sounds of the Sirens, stop them don't let them call me back with the sweetness of their sound, give me a rose to show how much you care and I'll give you a lock of silver hair, your sound for I have reached behind you, for the*

20. *Vor der Kaserne Vor dem grossen Tor Stand eine Laterne Und steht sie noch davor So woll'n wir uns da wieder seh'n Bei der Laterne wollen wir steh'n Wie einst Lili Marlene. Unsere beide Schatten Sah'n wie einer aus Dass wir so lieb uns hatten Das sah man gleich daraus Und alle Leute soll'n es seh'n Wenn wir bei de Laterne steh'n Wie einst Lili Marlene. Schon rief der Posten, Sie blasen Zapfenstreich Das kann drei Tage kosten Kam'rad, ich komm sogleich Da sagten wir auf Wiedersehen Wie gerne wollt ich mit dir geh'n Mit dir Lili Marlene. Deine Schritte kennt sie, Deinen zieren Gang Alle Abend brennt sie, Doch mich vergass sie lang Und sollte mir ein Leids gescheh'n Wer wird bei der Laterne stehen Mit dir Lili Marlene? Aus dem stillen Raume, Aus der Erde Grund Hebt mich wie im Traume Dein verliebter Mund Wenn sich die späten Nebel drehn Werd' ich bei der Laterne steh'n Wie einst Lili Marlene.*

familiar, this is safety, I cannot not go back.[21] A computer
bag is slung over his shoulder, his hand steadies it, the
carousel moves, a mechanical horse with bells attached to its
mane moves past him, *this is a wild horse for who can own
the insubstantial, in most languages the word for slave and
domestic is the same, a domesticated horse, a toy slave,* his
suitcase is a little behind it, a black suitcase, a small suitcase
with a silver metal handle. He leans forward, his face close to
the belly of a man, he has to bend lower because the bag is
behind the horse, almost underneath it, he grabs at the bag
and pulls it close to him, the bells on the horse ring as his arm
touches it, brush past the animal, which is made of wood,
authenticity, is this real or velveteen, the man whose belly is
next to his face does not move, he looks down at him, *do you
own this space, you have a bad smell, there is no space but my
space, I am not afraid of you, you will not suffocate me with
your girth, I am fearless, I enjoy this illusion, it is agreeable, this
experience makes me audacious, my fearless chimera.* Volker
stands upright, the case is next to him, he pulls the handle
from a small enclosed pouch on the top of the suitcase, this is
so he can pull the suitcase behind him as all the other people
are doing, *who invented the pull out handle, a suitcase on
wheels, wheels that are suitable for flat concrete floors with no
holes in them, my father, for him there were no wheels, he would
carry the bag no matter how heavy, his bag, the bag of my
mother, my bag, my father invented the suitcase with wheels.*
Volker moves away from the people. In front of him, to his
side, behind him, they all walk. Three women from another
flight who all wear the same sparkling glasses *that slag who*

---

21. In Ovid's *Metamorphoses* the Sirens are given magical wings by
Demeter, the fecund earth goddess, when she finds out that her daughter,
Persephone, has been abducted by Hades. She wished to create the perfect
seekers to search for Persephone. Then, when the Sirens do not intercede
with Hades, Demeter, in her grief, curses them. Sirens, the Muses of the
lower world, always beckon us to hell with a song that is irresistibly sweet.

would not bring me more wine, wore walk ahead of him, they too walk with a purpose, they pull their small carry-on bags behind them and hold the metal handles tenaciously, they are going somewhere. The bird encircled in a circle still flies, *cranes seldom fly, they are motionless and captured, their wings are clipped, they are no longer birds who believe that they are gods, these are fictional birds, endangered,* the three other women who walk with her also have birds that fly, or attempt to fly, on their chests, but they also cannot move for they are constricted in the blue cotton of the uniform, a sewn on stationary pattern, *one day I'll fly away, the ultimate romance, come what may, a green fairy sardonically satirises the ecstasy of dance, Baz Luhrmann likes the parody, as he likes the saturnine Nicole.*[22] Two men, both of whom wear peaked caps that hide their eyes, walk next to the women. Volker looks at them, they look tired for they have studied the aeroplane dials for a long time, *autopilot,* now they are tired and still have to both sleep and have sex with the airline stewards. Volker walks, he follows this flock of birds four women and two men, behind him he pulls his bag, it is not heavy so he does not have to strain. He walks slowly, the naturally red brown headed woman and the red blond child are still in a hurry, the woman runs past him, again, the child, whose feet still drag across the floor, looks at him, *all I want to do is hurry along the road to happiness, I hate this speed, it makes me nauseous, I want to vomit, where are we going to, she does not tell me, I hate the smell of new blood.* The child stares at him as he is dragged past, his expression is wistful, *you are slow, you do not speed, where is it that you go to, may I come with you, I want to be with you, I believe in you, I want you, I want to experience you*

---

22. *Moulin Rouge* is a jukebox musical directed by the Australian writer, director and fashion aficionada Baz Luhrmann. It tells the story of Christian, played by Ewan McGregor, a young English poet, who falls in love with the courtesan Satine, played by Nicole Kidman, the star of the Moulin Rouge cabaret theatre.

on your terms, it is impossible to experience anyone except in the world's terms, then I will experience you in the world's terms, I do not know myself as I do not know the world, he wants his life to move slowly, but the woman has somewhere to go. Volker stops and wipes his forehead, it is hot in the building, the terminal has an automatic heating system that purrs mechanically, there is no one below stoking a fire, there is no fire, just the mechanical hum of heat, he wipes his forehead with the material of his parka, then he stops, it is too hot, he takes the parka off, he folds it over his left arm, this is cooler, the sweat trickles from beneath his armpits and wets the white vest that he wears under his red jersey, but the stain is not visible, *sweat, the most authentic of human physicality must be disguised, I am afraid to take off my jersey for then the sweat stains under my arms will be visible, disgusting, all will be able to see that I am hot, I sweat, I am a man, we clothe our smell, our liquid salt in real smells, the fragrance of Dior, nature is dependable, marketable, faithful and always trustworthy, my smell is a collection of fragrances, I am a collection of images,* it is covered by layers of clothing, layers of material clothe the body, *silk is genuine, layers of emotion clothe the imagination, I cannot imagine where it is that I am going to, the red desert in a picture book, the reality of the appearance, the picture, the appearance is truth, in the spectacle I am undeceived, I cannot be mistaken for this is reality, a façade, a manifestation of somewhere, far away, I cannot touch it.* On his head is a woollen cap, this is also too warm for the inside space but he does not remove it, it is grey, a somewhat grey, somewhat blond fringe of hair lies across his forehead, it thrusts out from under the woollen cap, it lies flat, wet with his sweat. His eyes are blue. The line of people now move from the moving carousel and walk beside him, in front of him, behind him, he walks, once again he follows, edges closer, moves behind, he is a follower in this heated terminal for he has only a destination, no direction, he moves for others move, there is nothing else that he can do but keep on moving. The sweat under his arms is cold in the heat. The people move forward. Past a tobacconist on the right, the sign on the door *no smoking*, NO SMOKING, past the duty free almost supermarket, middle-aged man at the Thierry Mugler counter close to the entrance waves a bottle of A*Men Angel perfume, Volker knows this bottle for she wears it, and so once, did he, she gave it to him as a present, a birthday present …

THIERRY IS A friend of both Claudine and Jim/Peter. They both like him, albeit for very different reasons. Peter likes him because he works in the perfume and cosmetic duty free shop that is close to the curio shop, where he works. Jim/Peter often walks across to talk to him. They like to drink cognac together, a cognac in a bar, the Jolly Roger, where people can smoke. Thierry is a smoker. He likes to smoke with Claudine, and now, as he knows Jim/Peter, who is always in the vicinity of the duty free shop, more with Jim/Peter than Claudine because Claudine is usually in the sky. And Jim/Peter is very sexy, in a jaded elderly way. Smoke binds people together, as does cognac.

And Claudine, she loves perfume. Thierry always allows her to spray the testers on her arms and neck lavishly. So she goes into the shop whenever she is able to. Thierry, before he was employed in the duty free cosmetic and perfume shop, was known as both a visual and fragrance artist. He likes to believe that he perceives the space he is in through all his senses. He hears the river current, water tumbling over rocks, a distant car, the sound of the motor is loud and then it softens, it needs more power and so it accelerates, stops, the sound of the wind that hovers in the trees and blows the leaves to the ground. He smells the lost smoke of a burned-out cigarette, it settles into the room, it clothes the printed cushions in silver. He feels the wood of the table beneath his fingers, smooth as the feel of the skin on an inner thigh is smooth, untouched by the sun. He tastes the salt of his sweat, a vanilla mountain.

But Thierry cannot hear and he cannot smell. He knows that he, we all do, lives in a retinal society; sight is valuable, much more valuable than smell or touch; we look, we do not hear, we look and do not smell, we look and do not touch. He knows, because now that he can only use his eyes, that sight distances; the eye cannot see your smell, cannot hear your smell. He looks at people and objects, they are far away, he does not lean out and touch them, he does not smell their closeness; he does not listen to the ant that walks across the table. And so he remembers the corporeal stories of a time when he had these faculties; and his memories are imagined and distilled and created over and over again so that the words stay, the words that he tells Claudine and Jim/Peter. And because he has words, the words of a fragrance, the words of music, no one knows of his sensual lack.

And because he used to be a perfumer, he has smelled many aromas, created them, described them so many times, the sweet tuberose, as sweet as the oboe's sound, green as the prairie, fresh as a child's caress, rich, corrupt and profound, that he is uncertain whether he actually remembers the smell, or whether he remembers just the words, they loiter indolently in his imagination. The word frankincense, a gift to a king, rich, diverse, and opulent, the musk rat, the cigar, Cohiba, the photograph of a white dove that closes its wings as it sits on the shoulder of Fidel Castro, the smell of his mother's hair, the way the wind blows across an apartment at the ocean, a faint smell of the colour purple, the purple lily, or is it a cherry blossom; the smell weaves its way over the sky, a faint smell of peppermint mixed with the fumes of a bus.

And he remembers his smell, he smells his terror. It lingers for a long time. But this he does not tell Claudine and

Jim/Peter, this is his secret smell, the smell words cannot describe.

Thierry is a creator, a designer of future memories and anticipated pasts. And who would know that he does not smell or that he does not hear, least of all Claudine and Jim/Peter, although Jim/Peter suspects it because he has noticed that Thierry never answers him when he does not look at him.

THIERRY SPRAYS PERFUME on anyone who asks him to, but Volker does not want to smell this perfume, *memories are only stories, a smell makes the story sensual, why do I want to smell this perfume, I do not want this story.* Volker feels uncomfortable so walks towards the carousel where his luggage went around and around, where people waited for luggage that would never arrive. Next to it is a built-in desk, above it are words in many languages, the one that he understands says INFORMATION. On the desk there are several piles of brochures, one of them is a map of the building, a map of all the terminals of the Charles de Gaulle[23] airport. The airport is made up of three terminals;[24] Volker is in Terminal 1, he knows that he

---

23. This airport is a memorial to Charles de Gaulle. Memorials – we develop them, we erect them, we pay homage to them. We wear our memory lightly, it is somewhere outside of us. Our memories are our art, a statue made of cold grey stone.

24. There are three terminals that make up the airport: Terminal 1 is the terminal that Volker is in. Terminal 2 is broken into a number of different terminals, each distinguished by an alphabetical letter; this is the terminal where non-European aircraft discharge their passengers, aircraft from Africa, Asia or other such continents that are not Europe, or that are not North America, continents that do not fall within a world frame of reference, dark places that never grow cold. The letters of the alphabet correspond to different airlines. Terminal 2C is where the aircraft from Namibia arrive and depart. Terminal 3 is under construction.

needs to be in Terminal 2C at least two hours before his flight will depart, this is what the information on the boarding pass tells him, and, if the information on the boarding pass is correct, this gives him at least another ten

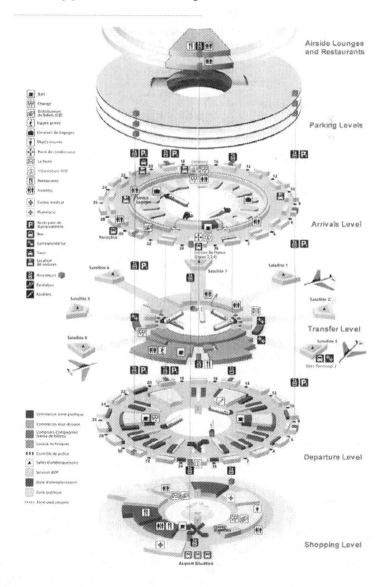

hours of waiting, *waiting, waiting,*[25] *I wait in unstructured time, if only I could know that in one hour I will have coffee, I will definitely have a coffee, if only I know that she will arrive, she will come back to me, look at the hands on the watch, they move.* Volker does not stop at the duty free shop, he walks past Thierry with his perfume, *why punish myself with a smell,* then he walks past a curio shop, also on the right, African curios, *authentic works of art and curios, pioneers of the materialist view of art.* He stops, walks back, after all he is going to Africa, he is travelling to Namibia, he goes into the African curio shop, people surge past him *an unbound river. An African curio shop in this airport, an African shop in the Paris airport, cheap African curios bought at a cheap airport gift shop, authentic African curios, no fakes here, individual works of art, there is no artist and the individual is a construction, we are all individuals, who is Picasso anyway, always individuals, what is distinctive, peculiar, talk to me of originality and I will turn on you with rage, I am a crowd, a lonely man, I am nothing? I am on my way to Africa, Namibia, Africa, so large and yet I can only say Africa. These curios are for people who have recently left Africa and have forgotten to buy a gift for someone, some inconsequential person who they know is consequential; a mother, a brother, I am on my way to Africa, somewhere other, somewhere strange, somewhere foreign, I know so little that I cannot even romanticise it, my emotions are pre-packed, my romance is a performance, I will always tire of the theatre, I will watch the lighted stage forever, the light will never fade.* Volker is on his way to Africa so he does not need to buy something for

---

25. In *A Lovers Discourse* Roland Barthes says: Am I in love? Yes, since I am waiting. The other one never waits. Sometimes I want to play the part of the one who doesn't wait; I will try to be busy, be elsewhere, to arrive late, but I always lose at this game. Whatever I do I find myself there, with nothing to do, punctual, even ahead of time. The lover's fatal identity is precisely this. I am the one who waits.

someone whom he has forgotten; still he walks into the shop. He walks down one of the three aisles, the shop has many things in it, African things, they come, these objects, from everywhere, China, Senegal, South Africa, India, *Africa is a large continent, it has over 900 million people who are all starving and dying and emigrating and complaining and Africa is a gigantic continent, Namibia is Africa: Africa has sunsets: Namibia is Africa, Namibia has sunsets over the desert and over the ocean and over the petrified forests, Africa has deserts and water and oceans and deserts and water and oceans, Namibia is Africa, Namibia has deserts and water and an ocean, Africa is a continent of endless possibilities, African souls are persecuted and prophetic souls. Am I?* He stops at a bookshelf, he reads some of the titles, Ras Makonnen and Arthur Rimbaud – The Story of a Romance that Could Never Be, Cheney & Botha – Diamond Mining in the Democratic Republic of Congo: How to Be a Successful Entrepreneur in Africa, Peter Beard – Islands of Morning, Peter Beard – The End of the Game. He bends down and takes a guide book from the shelf, *Africa is too large for generalisations. Africa is never too large for generalisations, Africa has fifty-four nations, five time zones, seven climates, 900 million people and 14 million stories, darkness, safari, big sky, primordial, Africa has no well-adjusted people anywhere, nowhere, never ever.* On the shelf above the guide books is another book, on the cover is a sunset, brown trees that have no leaves on them are silhouetted in front of the bright orange, *Orpheus[26] dances in the underworld, the world's*

26. In this story, as written by Virgil, Orpheus is deeply in love with his wife, Eurydice. Eurydice, on her wedding day, was attacked by a satyr. In her efforts to escape the satyr she fell into a nest of snakes and was fatally bitten on the heel. She died in the long grass, clothed in her wedding dress. Her body was discovered by Orpheus who, filled with grief, played sad and mournful songs on his lyre so that all wept. On the advice of the gods, who empathised with his pain, Orpheus travelled to the underworld and with his music softened the hearts of Hades and Persephone, who agreed

greatest music maker, follow me, follow me, I cannot look
backwards for then you will die, I have softened the heart of
the world, I have softened the heart of the underworld just to
be with you and yet I look back, I look back and search for
someone, someone else, something that is not me, another
book that lies next to it shows a photograph of infinite
desert sand and on another is a picture of an elephant,
three-metre ivory tusks, *I can never look back, I will never*
look back. But he does not take any of these books from the
shelf, he takes the guide book. The cover of this book also
has a picture of the sunset on it, a waning sun, bright
shadows on a sand of red, he turns the book over, on the
back cover is an ocean, a silver beach, a bleached carcass,
he looks more closely at the picture, the carcass is white, it
is not very large, a metre from one end of the spinal bone
to the other, he can clearly make out the spine, the ribs, the
legs, there are four of them, there is no meat left on the
carcass, a skeleton, a seal, *seals swim in the ocean, seals*
dance in the ocean, the ocean is beneath the world,
unknown, all African seals have rhythm, the caption underneath the picture, The Lonely Death of a Black-Backed
Jackal: The Skeleton Coast of Namibia, *the Skeleton Coast,*
not a seal but a jackal, a predator. Above the ocean and the
white carcass on the white beach is a greasy sky, lead
clouds slung low, he turns the book over again, the desert
is bright and the sun is hot. The words on the cover of the
book, NAMIBIA, are written in blue. Volker turns, there is
a desk and a chair close by, he takes three steps towards the
chair, then he sits on the chair, it is warm, as if someone

---

to allow Eurydice to return with him to earth, on one condition: Orpheus
should walk in front of Eurydice and not look back until they both had
reached the upper world. He set off with Eurydice following, but, in his
anxiety, as soon as he reached the upper world, he turned to look at her. She
vanished for the second time, forever. And so Orpheus wandered with his
lyre, and wondered, and walked, forever, but he could never get her back.

has just left it, *the body is gone but the warmth stays, the warmth will always stay, grow cold, grow cold, please grow cold. I must remember that the scent of you is gone, lifted from the sheets, that you are not coming back, that is has not rained.* On the desk is a pile of white paper, an Apple Mac desktop computer, which is chained to one of the table legs, an open leather-bound book that does not look as if it is for sale, it is old and worn, *well-judged and sagacious,* and a pair of black-rimmed Giorgio Armani spectacles. *I like this desk, I can rest my head on it, I am tired.* Volker sits down, the chair is possibly, or possibly not, for those who need a long time to look at a book before they buy it, or, even if they do not buy the book, they will still sit on the chair and browse through other books, look at the pictures, wander the continent they are about to go to, or not go to, just dreaming of, or have just left, rest their feet and legs for the airport that they are in is large, it is spread out over a vast area of land. Again Volker takes the boarding pass from the top right-hand pocket of his parka, it is conspicuously white against the green, he looks at it, he checks it again, Departure 21h00, Terminal 2C, Gate 45. He has a long time to wait, more than half of the daylight, although he cannot tell whether it is day or night, there is always neon, *it is always daylight in this airport, I will never sleep,* he has a lot of time to find his way to Terminal 2C, *time costs $50.00 per hour, time is not worthy of expense, it is as worthless as the minutes that fly by.* He sits on the chair and stretches his legs out in front of him, he lays his head on the thick leather-bound book that is next to the Apple Mac computer, *this can be stolen, this is why it is chained to this desk, we can never be trusting of others,* should another person walk down the aisle they will have to step over his legs because the aisle is narrow and his legs are long, not that long, but long enough to stretch across the whole aisle. He is tired, he lies forward onto the desk. Then he sits up again and looks at the open page of the leather-bound book, he turns the pages, the first and second pages have a contents page and the name of the publisher written on them, he does not need to know the publisher so he moves quickly over this page, he does not want to look at the contents either, he just wants to browse the book in its entirety, not read the whole book from page one to the final page, but rather skim through it, but then he realises that it is a book about law, French law, *the Napoleonic codes*, and he does not want to read the law, neither does he want to concentrate as he would have to do because the book is written in French, he wants to understand where he is going to, so he opens the guide book instead. *Africa is never too large for generalisations, the fifty-four nations, five time zones, seven climates, 900 million people and 14 million stories are all the same, Africa is in my blood, I can hear her call to me, Africa has no well-adjusted people anywhere,*[27] *I can save them,* what the country looks like, how cold it is in the winter. He has read about Namibia before, many books, but always there is something new, something that he did not know, *I do not know where I am going to, I do not know why I am going to this place, this is the underworld and I cannot even play the lyre.* He reads the words of the preface, *each African country is unique, Namibia is unique, it has less than two million residents and has never been through a civil war. While it was a part of the South African apartheid protectorate there was war, a guerrilla war ... The South West African Peoples Organisa-tion (SWAPO) ...* He realises that he has read this book before, it is the same book that he has in his suitcase, it is

27. This is how to write about Africa, use all the clichés, says Kenyan writer Binyavanga Wainaina in an essay published by Granta in 2005. The essay was then published as a little book by the Nairobi publishing house Kwani that was set up by him. Binyavanga no longer writes about Africa as he died of many things in 2019.

not immediatcly accessible to him but he knows that he put it in the suitcase, underneath the five shirts and next to his toiletry bag. He gets up from the chair and puts the book back on the shelf, *this is my destination, it is this country, this place that I do not know, this place that I will never know because I will choose not to know it, I will be a stranger, and yet my language is there, my language, the language that I know, I will have a community and yet I will be alone, I will go to the edge of the world.* He slowly looks around, then he walks back down the aisle, he turns a corner and walks down another aisle. In front of him, but quite far away, about ten metres, is the check-out counter. A clean-shaven older man with sprawling blond hair, *why would someone so old want to work in an airport shop,* is talking to a man who looks to be of Middle Eastern extraction, he is dark and has a beard, a turban is wrapped around his head. The older man gestures, holds the other man's arm, laughs, they know each other well. Then the man who looks to be Middle Eastern begins to walk towards Volker, he passes him but makes sure they do not touch, *the infidel is unclean,* and moves towards the desk and chair. He sits down and picks up the spectacles, he takes a pen from the right-hand pocket of his loose-fitting jacket, then he bends down and begins to read from the book, he stops to make a note on a piece of paper, then he continues to read, then he opens the Apple Mac computer, types in a few words, grunts and continues reading. Volker keeps walking. On his right is a stand that is covered in necklaces and bracelets and keyrings, they are all made from different beads, he thinks that the beads must come from a number of different countries, he picks up a necklace and looks at the label, *made in South Africa: African trade beads,* he moves towards the bead stand and puts out his hand, his fingers touch a keyring, *I want to feel Africa, I want to touch something that is African, maybe not the Africa that I am going to, but I must touch, touch is real,* tangible, *I touch her, a keyring for the keys that I no longer have for the apartment above the street.* Volker holds the keyring for a long time, *shall I, no, yes, why not, no, I do not need a whim, I am a consumer, consumers are everywhere, customers, I am not a consumer, I do not want this keyring for I have no keys, but I have the appearance of a key, the image of a key, a key to the room where she with the silver hair sits, I have a spectacle of her, my bond is mediated by the image of the key, and of her silver hair.* He walks further down the aisle, to his left is a clothes rack, there are a number of T-shirts on it, many of them have words on them, English, French, German, pictures of the wild animals of Africa, a green springbok holds a golden rugby ball, higher. The floor is green tiles, *grasslands,* he drags his feet across it, *I do not know how to be indifferent, this makes me susceptible to pain, I can feel hurt, my limbs are painful, I can feel the hurt.* He puts his hand into the pocket of his trousers, his fingers feel a book, a notebook, his fingers touch the pages that are empty of writing, an air ticket, Frankfurt–Windhoek, there is no return, *is there no writing, there is nothing to write, no writing, no writing, no writing, I am leaving the space of words, writing, leaving the space of everything speak-able, the bitterness of the world, I have nothing to come back to, I am not alone I am hiding, I cannot be alone for I will never go back to someone, I do not know words.* The African curio shop now fills up with people, ten minutes ago there was no one in the shop except Volker and the older shop assistant man and the Middle Eastern man. Volker looks at the shop assistant more closely now, his hair is blond and his skin is lined, he is tall and sinewy and thin, taut, when he was young some would have called him beautiful, *I wish I was thin, have run on the treadmill, I am a hamster on a wheel always with somewhere to go for what is movement, just the movement of going nowhere, we're on the road to nowhere.* On the counter next to the older shop assistant is a book,

Eyelids of Morning, it is open and as Volker passes by he looks at its open page. There is a signature on it, Peter Beard,[28] and the shop assistant, who looks like an older version of the young Peter Beard in the picture, looks at him; his younger persona has his thin legs in the mouth of a crocodile, *feed him, feed him* …

JIM IS A shop assistant who dresses in khaki, khaki shirt, khaki short pants, a khaki uniform. He looks, if one is not that close to him, like an older version of Peter Beard. Jim likes Peter Beard, his books, his machismo, his sexiness. He sometimes even calls himself Peter, he likes to pretend to the customers in the shop that he might just be Peter Beard. Jim also likes to smoke. He smokes as he has always enjoyed smoking, and Peter Beard smoked, a lot, and always where he went, where he lived, everywhere actually in the whole world, he could smoke. Now, in this shop at the airport he cannot smoke, unless he asks Mehran, his friend who, because he lives in the airport, spends long hours studying in the shop to take care of it if Jim or Peter goes out. He looks up at the air in the shop, it is recycled, the lights are neon, the African curiosities are curios, and he remembers when he could smoke just about anywhere. And so most of his time is spent either pondering about smoking or talking to Mehran about smoking, and Africa, where Mehran has never been, or, sometimes, when Mehran will stand in for him, he goes out to smoke with Claudine, an air stewardess for

---

28. Peter Beard is an American adventurer, hunter and photographer. He hunted with Bors von Blixen, Finch Hatton and Roosevelt. He fucked every model who posed for *Vogue*. Peter Beard lived and worked in Kenya for many years. Now, after a stroke and as he is an old man, he lives in New York and Montauk. He is the author and photographer of *Eyelids of Morning* and *The End of the Game*, which remain the standards for natural history reporting, stunning wildlife photography, cutting-edge ecological ideas, and hard-core realism. Peter Beard introduced Iman, the Somali model, to David Bowie at the Oasis Hotel in Lake Turkana.

Lufthansa whom he recently met at the perfume counter in the duty free shop. Thierry, also a friend, works in this shop with perfume, it is not far from the curio shop so Peter, or Jim, often goes in there just to talk, to tell his stories.

Smoking. He knows that it is always talked about: the cancerous effects of tar, someone wants to smoke, or wants no one else to, or maybe people just talk about relaxation and smoking.

Peter, or is it Jim today, watches a man walk down the aisle, he looks as if he could be a smoker, and because he wants to smoke right now he wonders if this man also wants to smoke, he looks like a smoker, his fingers may be stained.

Peter, for it is Peter today, likes to think of himself as a man of words as well as images, that ephemeral wisp of grey, while it may disappear quickly and leave an aroma behind, while it is lingering in hair or curtains acts to fill up a space, for the space without the smoke would otherwise be empty. And this shop is empty, empty of the smoke that should fill it. Peter looks at the man as he passes, he looks at the book that is on the check-out counter next to him, books, his book, *Islands of Morning*; he had many of his fashion wildlife photographs in books, he wants to tell this to the man but he does not. Now he just looks up at the unreadable air, smoke rising from the lighted end of a cigarette, his fantasy, it gives the room volume, substance, aroma. Yes, smoke defines space, it dances in it. It flows into all the fiddly little interstices and creates an evanescent cast of what is forever not; small sculptured angels that take ballet lessons in the air. Space, it has no use if there is no smoke, it is large and smokeless, a vacuum, smoke will fill it, the space is used. And there is no smoke in this airtight shop.

Smoke is like life, he thinks, life fills the void of being alive, as the smoke fills space. And, like life, smoke just is, it does not grow and change and gain meaning, it is and then it is not. The foolish comfort themselves and think that in life one keeps growing, that life will become rich and deep. But he knows that it is not like this. It is more like smoking. As the smoke fills the void with the first few strands of silken string, it looks wonderful, tastes wonderful; it is always there, will never be used up, will never end. Then the smoke moves on, the cigarette has burned down, there is an acrid taste. Yes, smoking is like living, it is a habit, it is always going to be given up, but never is; like life, it just goes right on living. And Peter, definitely Peter, always thinks of giving up smoking, and he never does. God is a Havana smoker, he smokes to put some space between him and the world, but even God is no longer allowed to smoke in most spaces. God is dead for he can no longer smoke, we have killed him – poor old Fred he smoked in bed.

At the door of the shop the man stops, Peter, for Peter and not Jim can tell a story, looks at him and calls out, calls out to all who are there. The man turns around, stops, waits and listens, as do several other people.

Gather round, please gather around, let me tell you my story.

The people in the shop stop, they close the book that is in a hand, they stand still and watch the performance.

Peter, that is my name, a name, a common name, it has no meaning unless you are of the Christian faith, then I denied Christ three times. Denial, oh yes, it is my favourite pastime. I am cunning, I always forget my defeats. I deny that they ever happened. I forget that I am in this shop, and surely I have never been defeated, I adapt to do everything I want to do again, and then again. I take photographs. I was a fashion photographer, celebrated in New York, London and Paris. I was favoured by Veruschka. My photographs were printed in *Vogue* and *Vanity Fair*. Veruschka, she loved the photographs that I took of her cradling the neck of a giraffe or strung out, and over, a dead elephant. I was also a wildlife hunter. I hunted with Roosevelt and Hemingway, and I flew small planes with Beryl Markham and Denys Finch Hatton. I fucked Beryl Markham,

but then she fucked everyone so that's not much to boast about.
I left a mark, always a mark, on everyone I met. Cain's mark.
But this is now just a memory, an out-of-print memory of the
past, a record of the present, an image of the future. Picture an
elephant reaching for the last branch of a tree, a vestigial giraffe
plodding out of the picture, its legs lost in mirage. Do you
want to buy the book? Look – Taschen publishes it now. You
can display it on your coffee table. There were wild parties at
Montauk (it's just outside New York), with guests … Who were
they? I can't remember. I was too drunk, too stoned. Now I
work in this airport shop. Why – I must remember this – why?
For another kind of experience, to understand the traveller as
I am a traveller, and I, I will never understand me. It is another
performance, another photograph, another mythic manifestation of no one but me. Or is it because I am no longer rich? I
blew all the money away on children and women and pleasure.
But I dream, at night, and sometimes in the day, of my stories. I
will tell you a story, a hunting story. Listen. Listen to me.

Jim picks up a book, *The End of the Game*, opens it and
begins to read.

I move the head and pull at the throat, taut, to look at
the moon. To the left and slightly below the orb is a star. It
is sunlight bright, a light year away. When I look at the sky
all perspective is relative, a trick, orange, the planet Mars. I
swivel my head to the right and look at the tail of Scorpio.
The sting is bitter, painful, deadly. I am unable to navigate my
stories. I have left the path. I wonder how long I will be lost.
I am in my time and my circumstance. When I look at the
sky I know that all the stars and all the planets are a myth,
living fairy tales, but not for me. Some are dead, dead pale
fires self-perpetuating in time and distance. But they cannot
exist alone; they must be created in my mythology. I cannot
preserve the living as the living cannot be a myth. My photographs are dead. A branch of thorns in the shape of hooks
catches my hair. The thorns catch a stray piece and reel me in

towards the sharpness. The tree trunk is bent. It leans to the east. The prevailing winds blow from the west. The sun rises in the east. The tree is bent into the shape of a bird, a crooked dove that escapes the shadow. I pull to discharge its terror and so stumble towards it. The more I pull the more the thorns pull me closer to the steel, a trap. I struggle and am caught, crowned again. A thin yellow brown dog of no obvious pedigree which has a long tail scratches the ground next to my boots. It can move. It can run. I cannot. I am caught by the tree of thorns. The brown dog runs backwards and forwards, into and out of the squat bush. It makes a sound that could be a bark caught in its throat, but it's not a bark. When it was a pup it was taught not to bark when out under the moon, so it does not bark at the moon as other dogs do. It is silent. I lift my head and look at the moon. It is full, the perfect night. I pull at a thread of hair and I am loose. I walk delicately through the bush. The yellow brown dog follows me. I lean over the wire. The head of the bushbuck moves and looks at me, or it looks at the moon, or at the forgotten stars. Its eyes are glazed. I hate the taste of meat. It is not sweet even when it is basted with honey. I take a pair of steel wire-cutters from the brown bag that hangs from my left shoulder; the sound is loud in the dead air. Snap. The head of the bushbuck sags towards its brown neck. I put a piece of rope around the body. The rope has steel picks attached to it and they catch in the fur. I reel it towards me. The dog licks the blood where the wire has cut into the neck. Fresh blood always smells of semen. I think this buck died a long time before I got here. The moon follows its orbital path, it crosses the sky westwards, a thorn moon shadow bisects my throat. I do not believe in ghosts, but this is a ghost, my ghost, my ghost of ghost stories. I am the ghost of Peter Beard.

Jim is no longer Peter. He remembers he is a shop assistant so he stops reading. He takes money from a customer, puts it in the till, places the item that has been sold in a brown paper packet. Then he begins to talk again. But he wants to be Peter, he wants it very badly, and so he cannot stop himself continuing with his story. I love the lore of Africa; the fiction, the illusion. I photographed it, its animals and its people. But I am here now for I took my photographs, photographs with the eyes of a man who believed in the African myth. The alive are not a myth; I can only preserve something that is dead. I am here, in this shop, I am dead. I am contemptuous of my craft, for I know that an artist can never believe in his art. I am an artist. I believe, as the Turkana do, that the earth is flat. I will die as I was born. Will I know, will I want to know, those blurred shadows that are memories? Will I want to understand a world in which the romance of my life is written? I think that I will never understand it, nor do I want to.

The Muslim man who sits and reads from the law book at the table at the back of the shop stops reading. He sighs. He has heard this story before and now it is disturbing his concentration.

And so now I work here, always busy, busy always to do something, not to be. My being can wait until tomorrow. God and the Devil are one, so listen to this story – how long do you have before you have to board your flight? Listen. Let me tell you a story. And why not buy that book, it's all about crocodiles, look at me: I am alive in that enormous mouth, ha, yes, you guessed it, the crocodile is dead, and here, the elephants … No, the hunter did not kill the elephant. The railroads did, the bisecting of their space.

Peter stops talking.

And Jim leans forward to take money, this time from a woman with red-brown hair who is slightly out of breath; a crying child stands next to her. Peter looks at the boarding pass for the aeroplane that the woman will get on later. He hands her the change and puts the stuffed nylon elephant into a brown paper bag and gives it to her. She leans down and hands it to the child, who wipes his eyes and smiles.

The Muslim man lowers his head.

SHALL I FORSAKE the love of women for food? Can I tear the meat from the bone, the limb from the torso? Shall I abandon her for she has abandoned me? Yet I must eat. I am special, but no one is special, so how I can be special with nobody being special, I cannot solve this problem, leave it to the experts, the logicians, I must forswear this love for she is dead, I will take another as a lover, all women will despise me for I am me. Volker stands in the doorway of the shop and looks around him. He walks closer to the stand on which there are many beaded keyrings, he places the keyring back on its metal stand. The older man who is the shop assistant is talking, he gives a performance for now the shop is filled with people, those that are going to Africa and who want to know what it is that they may find there, those that have just returned and have forgotten to buy something for a consequential person, or none of these things, *I have thought this before, it was written before I was able to choose my thought,* just people who have nothing better to do, nowhere that they need to go to. He stops talking to attend to a customer, Volker recognises the woman who ran past him earlier, the woman and the child, they stop to pay for a curio they have bought. Another flight has arrived, the people in the shop are warmly dressed and their faces are pale, there is only one black man in the crowd; the black man, too, is warmly dressed, *stereotypes are so valuable, I can recognise them, black is the outsider.* Volker leaves the shop without buying the guide book on Namibia. *Where is the keyring, it is in my pocket, I have stolen a small thing, a keyring, property is theft and I want to lock up all my possessions for I know that I am a thief, we are all thieves, we steal identity, what is my name, I am a manic detective, Berg?*[29] Volker has no need for the book as he has the book, it is in his

---

29. Berg is a character from a book by Ann Quin, an English Beat writer who killed herself by walking into the sea at Brighton. And he (Berg) came to the town to kill his father.

suitcase, and he is going to Namibia anyway, he will look at the pictures that are not pictures, he will stand on the yellow sand of the desert and watch the sun setting in the sky, *an oasis of horror, there is no water, what time will the sun set in Namibia, in a desert of boredom, will it set at the same time as it sets in Frankfurt, will it be cold, what is the time in Namibia, time is my invention, I am waiting for my destiny.* He hunches his shoulders and pulls the parka closer to him, it still hangs over his arm, *hot, hotter, my memory is of a cold winter day in Berlin, the many cars, the many people walking to somewhere, the many layers of snow on the pavement, the cold sweat that I like to lick, to lick from her body, but in my actions, in my thoughts, in what I did, there was a flaw, an original flaw which was to need her silver hair, she who did not need me. Did I resist this flaw, or did I know in my heart that all resistance would be lost; it was always intended to be lost. I knew that I would lose, but to imagine that there would be a loss was not a thought that I wanted to entertain, the one I wanted was to believe that I would never lose, and so there was an accident due to my carelessness. The idea that I would never lose her was not an error, but a postponement of indisputable knowledge, and now this thought is a form of idiocy, for I have lost.* Volker reaches into his top right-hand pocket and takes out his boarding pass, he looks at it again to make certain what terminal he should go to, Terminal 2C, and the time the flight is to leave at, *time, time, time, important time, my time is over for nature knows no time, my time runs by, a marathon man, a practical man.* The green parka beats against his thighs as he walks. He walks further forward, then he looks at his watch, the time on the watch is 13h30, he has a digital watch so as to be able to tell whether it is night or day for in this building the neon lights are always on, they never close down, *nature knows no time, time is a construction, the architectural design of this airport, this memorial to immortality, Charles de Gaulle. Who is this man, this man who is the same as I am a man, this design constructs my thought for there is no time, and there is no man called Charles de Gaulle, he has left the world for the universe that is indifferent to him, I cannot and will not know him, he is a spectacle of what is just, just is.* A sign, it is covered in small black letters, it is laminated and pasted onto the white wall next to a box that looks as if it has electricity cables in it, *that has electricity cables, a snake, a viper bites the heel of Eurydice, I cannot find her silver hair in the underworld without this electric light, without the electricity cables, without a torch,* they are enclosed in metal, isolated and insulated, reads: Should there be a power outage the fifteen Hoover generators will immediately switch on, this is automatic, Terminal 1 will always be light. *It is a permanent day, a Beautiful Day, a 24 hour day and another 24 hour day of light and 24 more, no ending is not beautiful, it was a beautiful day reach me I know I'm not a hopeless case.* He looks in front of him, then he looks left, a metre to his left, he moves his eye left so as to be able to read the sign above the kiosk, it is too far away for him to make out the actual letters so he walks towards it, the sign has arrows on it and words indicating places to go to: walk 500 metres, 5 minutes, turn left, walk 300 metres, 3 minutes, turn right, and then two words in capital letters, SALLE A MANGER/FOOD HALL. So much space, *distance referred to in kilometres, space referred to in time, 3 minutes, 300 metres.* He will follow the directions on the signboard that is on the front of this kiosk as he wants to smoke, to drink, to eat. There is no one in the kiosk, only a number of computer terminals that are chained to nails, or knobs, on the wall. Then a small bald man, *a man of restricted height, he has black hair on his face,* he is dressed in a clown suit, red and yellow spots on a white suit, *clowns,*[30] *a clownish*

---

30. A clown is a conundrum. In a circus a clown makes the audience laugh, in a horror movie a clown makes the audience fear. A clown is never just a person who has a family, a love affair, the happiness and distress and anxiety and glory that most all people experience.

*condition, happiness is a clownish condition, miniature men
are tolerated they are no longer subjected to that easy ridicule
of my boyhood, my thoughts are idiotic, clownish, why do I use
this word clown in such a pejorative way, clown, idiot, clown
idiot,* walks up to the kiosk. *Only the stupid are not depressed,
happiness is a clownish condition, my thoughts are idiotic, I
have a flaw, my flaw was to need you with silver hair who did
not need me.* Volker stands still and watches the dwarf clown
enter the kiosk. The clown has no hair on his head but he has
hair on his face. He takes out a card, *plastic money, money is
fake, a commodity that exists for its own sake, there is no
money only plastic, where are the silver nuggets, the thirty
pieces of silver that were paid for my betrayal, everything here
costs money, what can thirty pieces of silver buy, directions to a
SALLE A MANGER/FOOD HALL, a machine to capture all
your data, a sleeping chair, how many pieces of silver will I take
to sell my soul, let the devil take it for free, this is hell.* The
diminutive clown reaches up, he attempts to hold what looks
like a passport underneath the barcode reader on a computer,
but he cannot reach it, the clown looks vexed, his mouth
smiles but it is bitter, it is painted upon his face, his lips are
red and wide, *injected with collagen for clowns must always
smile,* there is no step for him to climb onto in order that he
may reach the computer terminal. Volker watches the clown,
he bends down and turns his suitcase on its side, then he
climbs onto the suitcase, *do you imagine that I am a five-year-
old genius, I will never give you an inch, I am an
achondroplastic dwarf,*[31] *I am a clown.* The suitcase sways

---

31. Disproportionate dwarfism is characterised by one or more body parts
being relatively large or small in comparison to those of an average-sized
adult. Proportionate dwarves are midgets. Clowns are almost always disproportionate dwarves. The most common form of dwarfism in humans
is achondroplasia. It produces short limbs, increased spinal curvature, and
a distortion of the skull; a dwarf's limbs are shorter than his body, and his
head is enormous, in relation to his shortness, as it is a normal adult size.

under his weight for, although he is small his body is wide and the bones of his small frame are big, his head is large and his limbs are short, he is heavy, *I am a clown, I am a clown, the regular alliance of happiness with idiocy is one of the world's most painful features, and I am happy, always happy, always smiling, my smile is a painted smile,* and now being able to he reaches up and holds the passport under the reader and then, once it has been scanned, begins to type the numbers of the credit card that he holds on the keyboard. He stops to read something on the screen, then he presses a button, he reads, he waits, he presses another button, the machine begins to buzz, a piece of white paper emerges from a slot that is situated just below the keyboard, he takes the piece of paper from the machine then he climbs off his suitcase, takes it by its silver handle and walks away, *a robot miniature man.* Volker walks closer so as to be able to read the directions that are on the wall, he looks inside the kiosk at the computers, a sign tells him that they are there to record the tax refund amount that can be obtained should someone buy goods for which he can claim such a refund, *expensive Parisian goods.* The man, who is small, can now claim his refund. *What did he buy in Paris, a Vivienne Westwood[32] shirt, perfume by Thierry Mugler, A*Men, an AK-47, he has real balls, real Rheims[33] champagne?* Volker stops, he reads the words on the sign, then he walks on for 5 minutes, 500 metres, he turns left, he walks for 3 minutes, 300 metres and then he turns right. He follows the clown, who drags his suitcase, the floors of the airport are even, the suitcase rolls

32. The Vivienne Westwood shop in Paris is situated at 175 Rue Saint Honore. Vivienne Westwood dressed Sid Vicious until the day he died; this was not for long as he died young.

33. Rheims is the centre of champagne production. No sparkling wines made anywhere else can be called champagne, if not made in Rheims. Jean Baudrillard lived in Rheims for a long time, until the day he died, and he was old when he died.

along easily, the clown does not trip or fall, and neither does the suitcase. Volker watches the clown until he disappears into one of the bars, or is it a restaurant? Volker stops and waits, in front of him is a large space that is filled with people and eating houses, some of the places are open, a counter with pictures of various foods above it, the picture and the price, *the picture is airbrushed and always looks better than the food that is served,* others are enclosed, the signs outside most of those that are enclosed have the word ALCOHOL on them, many of them also have a small picture of a cigarette, the cigarette does not have a line drawn through it, the sign means that within the closed space a person may smoke. *So hot, alcohol will cool, alcohol cools the senses, deranges the senses as words can derange the senses, people in Paris smoke, Germans smoke, I smoke, I am unaware of the health warnings, Parisians are unaware of the health warnings, life is smoking a cigarette, the first few drags taste wonderful, the cigarette will never end, it can never be used up, I am alive, why don't I give it up? Life is a habit, I always say that I will give it up and I never do. I want to smoke when I am flying above the earth, I want to live when I am on the ground, we all have cancer, I do not want to die a long and miserable death. Quick; stub out the cigarette.* He looks across to the food tables, he is standing slightly higher than the height at which the tables are placed so he looks down on many heads, heads that have hair on them, white, black, curls, straight, and sometimes heads with no hair, all the heads are semi-bowed, *praying to a god who is no longer here,* and all the heads have an imperceptible movement, the movement of masticating jaws, *a conveyer belt of moving muscles, we are all original, originality is always the same.* A man with a flat muscled stomach talks into his mobile phone, his stomach is exposed to show the tattoo of a San Francisco biker gang *that he does not belong to,* another stands close to him, he also talks into a phone, his large belly is exposed over the overhang of his belt to show the tattoo of the Los Angeles biker gang *that he does not belong to*, the necklace folds into skin, a neck brace, and a woman taps lightly into a phone, on her neck is a tattoo of the London biker gang *that she does not belong to. We are all the same but for the colour of our hair, silver hair, thirty pieces of silver, I cannot submit to this memory, I cannot for if I do not I will forget, memory as reference, an analogy, I will not betray my pain, my allegiance is to my history, the hole in the grain of many things, my history can fill this hole, as can any other story.* The heads appear to be far away from Volker, although they are in fact only a few metres in front of him. There are several closed doors opposite him, if he wants to reach them he must cross the food hall, to do so he has to step slightly downwards, the ground floor that he stands on is slightly higher than the floor on which the people, with their bowed heads, sit *and pray to a god who looks like them, a god who, for a price, will provide them with nourishment, succour.* At a table, halfway across the food hall is a child, he sits alone. Volker walks forward towards the bars in front of him, he has not yet chosen the one that he wants to enter, but as they are all in the same general direction he just walks towards them. He walks past the child, the child looks at him, he is motion-less, only his eyes move, *the child is searching for something, someone, is it me, why does he want to find me, no one can find me for I am lost, alone, I have no community therefore how can I be alone, I am hiding, I am lost, I am not lost, I am going to a bar to drink and smoke, I am going to a faraway land where the colour of skin is not my colour, where there is nothing that is the same, the land where the blue-throated sunbird is worshipped.* The child has red hands, red small hands, *how big is a child's hand, I am a man, I have hands that are big, my hands are the hands of a man that can grasp another around the throat, why are those hands so small, are they a child's hands?* The sex of the child is indeterminable for he, *he always encompasses the other gender, he is she, she is never he,* is wrapped up in a thick woollen brown coat despite the fact that it is warm inside the food hall in Terminal 1. On Volker's head is a red beret. On the chair opposite the child, Volker has, by taking at least twenty steps, moved closer to him, *it is a boy the masculine downturn of a mouth, men in repose never smile,* is a black bag, not a handbag but a carrier bag, an overnight bag, it has a long strap attached to it, on the table in front of the bag is a newspaper, the newspaper is open to the sports section, between the snaky black and white word a man jumps, *he jumps so high that he almost moves out of the pages, he almost jumps out of his clothing,* a soccer player, he lashes out a foot to catch a ball. *I will never meet this football player, I am too far away, I can only look at a picture, it resembles what it has captured, a football player, a body in space, he is black and dressed in red, everything around me is black.* The bag is closed. There is no one but the child at the table, *he is too alone, completely alone, waiting, he has been alone for a long time, does he write letters to others who are alone, as I do, I am watching myself for I too am alone, I watch a figment of my imagination, a calamitous attempt to revive a platitude, what am I waiting for but you. I will always wait. I will always be waiting. Am I in love? Yes, since I am waiting. The lover's fatal identity: I am the one who waits.* Volker walks past the child, as he does so the child reaches out his left hand, the hand touches Volker's trousers, *where are you going to,* the child does not speak, he cannot feel this touch for it is swift and soft and he is going to a bar for a cigarette and a beer, *did I hear you say something, was it you that spoke, no, I heard nothing except the voices of people, the hum or static on a radio.* Volker says nothing for no one has spoken to him, he continues to walk forward. *Watch me, watch me, watch me want you, but I will leave you.* He looks to the left and chooses a bar that appears to include food and alcohol, the sign next to the door has a picture of a bottle as well as a sandwich on it, it also has a picture of a cigarette, the smoke curls upwards towards the ceiling of Terminal 1, but the ceiling is so high that the smoke does not reach it, the ceiling is white not black or yellow, the smoke has not made a dent in its pristine non-colour. In front of the door to the bar is a vending machine, bottled mineral water and soft drinks can be bought from the machine should a person put a specific number of coins into it, the instructions on the machine are clear and outsize, no change, exact coins required, the water and the soft drinks are of varying prices. Many people stop at the vending machine to buy water, *unsullied water, what is so authentic about authenticity, water not tainted by chemicals, water is made up of chemicals, H_2O, is it pure, sinless, water for sale, goodness at a price, chemicals are everywhere, germs are everywhere, don't touch you will get sick, what is authentic water, authenticity is a fetish, new age, the virus will invade.* He stops at the machine and puts his hand into the pocket of his trousers, then he stops, takes his hand from his pocket, it would seem that he does not want to buy this virtuous water from the vending machine, *if I do not buy this water I am condemned to a life of inauthentic drinking, only the rich can be authentic, they pay for their water, the poor must forever be impure, sullied by their inability to pay for the real, real water.* He pushes the door to the bar, it swings forward, he walks into the bar and the door closes automatically behind him. For a moment he stops and looks around him. The bar is not full; probably only half a dozen of the tables have people sitting at them. At one of the tables is a man, he does not wear a shirt, it is hot in the bar, his chest is hairless, as is his head, a swastika in pink is tattooed across his skull, he holds his head in his hands as if he is in despair. At another is the man who sat next to Volker on the aeroplane, Volker recognises his T-shirt, Princeton Alumni. Then the man who was previously on the aeroplane gets up, he crosses the floor to the table where the man who has no hair sits, he reaches out and takes the man's hand as if to comfort him. The man does not take his hand away. The man wearing the T-shirt takes a tissue from the pocket of his blue tracksuit pants, he leans over to the man who cries and wipes the tears that run down his checks, and then he gives him the tissue so that he can blow his nose which is streaming mucus. At the bar counter itself are four people, two men and two women, all four of them are seated on bar stools. The women are silent, *a silent movie.* One of the women is older; she wears a white smock with the words Cleaner/Nettoyeur embroidered in green, *a slime dam,* onto the area just over her right breast. The younger woman, her hair is very red, almost scarlet, stares at the empty glass that she holds, then she squeezes it, the glass breaks and blood runs from her hand. The older woman leans over and holds out a roll of toilet paper so that she can take a piece from it to wipe the bar counter, and her hand, should she so chose. The men do not notice the broken glass, neither do they notice the blood; they are talking to each other. Volker cannot hear their words for he is too far away, they talk in hushed tones. *I will never hear them, I will never hear anyone.* The man closest to him has a dark black beard, he is thin and wears designer jeans, the buckle on his belt is made of inter-connecting Gs. *Gucci, we live in a collection of images, there is no way out.* He wears a white linen shirt, he is close, close to the other man. Volker looks at the other man, then he looks down at the ground, he looks for four sets of feet but there are only three, the man who sits next to the man with the black beard and designer jeans cannot reach the ground with his feet, his feet do not reach the bar across the bottom of the bar stool, *a miniature man, the clown, the miniature is a refuge as all people are clowns, what do clowns want in this airport, is he a spiteful, vindictive clown? Why do clowns make me afraid, what lies behind the painted smile? Does this clown fool me, do they all fool me, fool me, make a fool of me, once, shame on you, twice, fool me again, I can't get fooled again …*

KARL IS A terrorist, a terrorist clown, a terrorist dwarf, a terrorist with dwarfism. He grew up (the spiteful say he never grew up) in Brooklyn, New York. Karl is an American, an American terrorist. He has no cause but his own; he believes in the freedom of the individual, this is the American way. He is not a Muslim, a Christian fundamentalist or an Irish Republican, he does not even belong to a grouping of other dwarves who seek to create a social climate of tolerance and harmony for all dwarves by burning down anything that is not dwarf friendly, which is just about everything. He does not think about issues: why should dwarves not be allowed to marry tall people, the prevalent belief that all dwarves are homosexual pederasts (some are, Karl is not), etc. Karl is a terrorist in his own cause. A psychotherapist might say he has short man issues, he hates being looked down upon, he hates being laughed at, and most of all he hated it that his Grade Two teacher said that his only vocation was to be a clown.

But he took this advice seriously nonetheless, and when he was twenty-seven he did become a clown. He liked the make-up; for the rest it was merely a disguise. Initially he joined a circus, but then, once that novelty had worn off, and he had fucked all the other circus creatures, girls and boys and animals, he decided to leave and do something else. Although nowadays he still dresses as a clown, he never pretends that he still works in a circus. People just assume that he does because where else do clowns work, and so it is a good disguise. Karl's belief is the more you stand out in the crowd the less you are noticed, so being a clown is an excellent disguise for a terrorist. No one suspects a clown; clowns are not there, even though they are right under your nose. A clown is never just normal. Clowns are a conundrum: in a circus they create laughter; in a horror film fear. Karl enjoys creating fear. He has made this part of his persona.

Being a terrorist means that he has to go to many different parts of the world in pursuit of people to terrorise, so

Karl travels frequently. This is not difficult because he has money and can pay for all his airfares and train fares and even accommodation in the richer cities of the world. Tokyo: he had once collaborated there with a group who placed a lethal gas canister on the overpass that straddles Omotesando Street, one of the most sought-after fashion districts in Tokyo. The gas canister exploded, leaving three dead and twenty injured. Initially Karl was reluctant to participate in this act of terrorism because, being a lover of beauty, more particularly beautiful buildings, he knew that it was likely that the TODS building, designed by Toyo Ito,[34] would be damaged. Fortunately, it was not but this was because Karl, who knew about bombs and other incendiary devices, placed it far enough away to damage only people. As part of the mission he had the opportunity to walk up and down the street. He looked longingly at the clothes that would never fit him, and the people, who were small and smooth, and, of course, the buildings. And as he walked he thought how lucky he was to be a terrorist.

Karl wanted, above all, to be noticed. He wanted his fifteen minutes of fame. He did not want to go to jail – for a dwarf this could be murderous; he would be fucked up the arse by those much larger than him – but he did want to receive accolades in the terrorist world and be an occasional newspaper headline. Not that he himself ever was a headline but his

---

34. Toyo Ito is a Japanese architect. He designed TODS Omotesando Building in Tokoyo. As a representative of the Conceptual Architectural School, he seeks to express both the physical and the virtual worlds, a simulated city; a living fantasy. Everything is a simulation, a copy of a copy of a copy … So where is the real? It is nowhere; it has never been; it, too, is a simulation. Buildings are the clothes of the urban dweller. On the overpass that straddles Omotesando Street the TODS Building is a seductive space. What is one looking at – a tree through the transparent glass, or a reflection of a tree, and when two trees are lined up in relation to the glass one does not know whether there is a second tree, and even if it is a real tree, a metallic tree. The building is both an actor and a structure.

exploits were. He loved to read about them, show them to his terrorist colleagues.

The reason Karl is rich is interesting. When he was eighteen, as he was walking through Central Park, alone – he did not have a friend; who wants to befriend a dwarf? – he was noticed by an elderly widow, Carla Route Ely. She liked the look of his face. He was handsome in that dwarfish way. Carla was rich; she had inherited money from her mother, who in turn had inherited money from her father, who had inherited it from his father, who had made it in the subway business. She had also made a study of dwarves because her great-grandfather, from whom the money derived, according to her mother, had been a dwarf. In actual fact this wasn't true. Her mother and her mother's mother had made it up. They just liked the idea of having a dwarf in the family (both of them were fairly short). There were no photographs of her great-grandfather in the house but one, and this was only of his face, not his body. Carla's mother, and her mother, had taken care to cut the body out of this photograph.

Because Carla believed her great-grandfather was a dwarf she developed an interest in dwarves. First she set up a dwarf shelter in Brooklyn. Brooklyn was yet to be gentrified. It was still poor and dangerous, but only one person – and he was not even a dwarf, he was a midget; there were not many homeless dwarves in New York at the time and so a midget was as good as a dwarf – resided in this shelter. Then, fortuitously, she met and made friends with Karl. In the course of her long interest in dwarves she had gained a lot of knowledge: the types of dwarfism, famous dwarves and much other irrelevant and inconsequential information. Carla immediately knew that Karl was a disproportionate dwarf, but although his limbs were unexceptional, in fact grotesque, his face was extremely handsome. (Handsome is a relative term; to Carla, Karl was handsome.)

And so Carla and Karl used a lot of Carla's inherited

money to set up an elaborate worldwide terrorist network of dwarves (or most of them were dwarves; some were just dwarf friendly). This had been Karl's idea. He liked the idea of being a rich dwarf terrorist and persuaded Carla that her money would be better spent blowing up subways and buildings and people than running a homeless shelter in which there was only one resident who was not even a dwarf, but a midget. Karl convinced Carla that what he wanted most of all to do in life was promote the cause of all dwarves (even though he did not really want to do this, he only wanted to promote the cause of himself and have a good time doing it, and this meant he would have to be rich and therefore it was in his interests to know Carla). And as neither was harmed in this arrangement, it continued for as long as Carla was alive, which was only for six years after they met. But then, as she left him all her money (which was considerable as she had never married – she just liked calling herself a widow; it sounded far more acceptable than spinster) Karl was able to continue with what they had started. Carla died a happy woman.

And then, after Carla died, Karl joined the circus. He joined just for the hell of it, for the experience of knowing that while there is always a smile that is large and red painted on unhappy disfigured faces (clowns are always unhappy, much like caged animals are unhappy), but also because this was the perfect disguise. While he was part of the circus he built up the terrorist group and managed it on a part-time basis. Then, when this became too much for him (the organisation had grown), he left the circus to run it full time. He missed the circus, but not enough to go back to it. And being a terrorist paid off. In no time at all the organisation expanded to seismic proportions. It even had a branch in Kiev (the Ukraine was a hotspot for terrorism).

The secret to a good terrorist organisation, Karl realised early, was to have no cause at all but to support any cause

that happened to come up. So his, or his by now exten-
sive network, moved between gay rights to nationalism to
Nazism. He mostly worked in the left-wing human rights
arena, where there was more scope, there were more causes
(and much more money). Sometimes there were environ-
mental causes that needed his assistance.

Now he was in Paris to assist a Muslim grouping, most of
whose members were Sunni, of Algerian extraction. Many
had family who had been killed by the French in the war of
independence. But in fact Karl had been fooled (and this was
the first and last time that he would be). What he didn't know
was that the Sunni group consisted of one person, who really
only wanted to rescue his brother from the arrogant and big-
oted French, or as Mohammed liked to call them, the frogs.

THE SOUNDS IN the bar are very loud. Music plays from the
jukebox in the corner opposite the entrance, *it's been seven
hours and thirteen days since you took your love away I go out
every night and sleep all day since you took your love away.*[35]
The two women at the bar, the younger and the older, and
who are still silent, wear a lot of make-up, a slash of red down
the cheek, red lips, purple paint on watery eyes, it is as if
they have been over made up because they're in a movie or a

---

35. This song was written by Prince and performed live by him and Rosie
Gaines. Prince is known for his flamboyance and his view that life might
be a performance but his shows were just so much better. The *Los Angeles
Times* called Prince 'our first post-everything pop star, he defies everything
including the categories of race, genre and commercial appeal'. Prince was
a sex symbol for everyone, the androgynous, the amorphous, the trans,
the hipster; a queer icon, immortalised by Andy Warhol in his screen print
Orange Prince. He often dressed in purple, hence his song Purple Rain,
loved animals, hence this is the sound that doves make when they cry and
sadness, hence nothing compares 2U. In August 2017 Pantone Inc introduced a new shade of purple in their colour system in honour of Prince.
The shade is called Love Symbol #2 and is defined as Pantone colour number 19-3528.

television series. *The performance of their lives is dull.* They sit close to each other, *bored sisters, a mother and a daughter in it for the trick, prostitutes, the comfort of the simulated touch, I need the human touch, I want to fuck someone in the movies, construct the face in video paint, anyone, give me flesh, skin, warmth, I am poor, give me money.* The clown and the swarthy man still speak in hushed tones. *Will they plant a bomb? Are they secret police disguised as criminals? Sincerity is the denial of complexity, criminals are sincere, they are caught by those who are insincere.* All the people at the tables in the bar talk spiritedly to each other or, if they are alone they smoke energetically, for this is a smoking bar, most people come into it not to drink or to eat but to smoke for Terminal 1 has few such smoking venues. Volker approaches the bar. The man behind it, *ennui*, is bored. His face is dark, he is not of European origin, Moroccan or Algerian, he is not dark enough to be from lower down Africa, he is probably from the northern part of Africa, from where the former French colonies were. The barman is Semitic, his features are those of an Arab, *thick Arab, we have transferred our hatred of the Jews to the Arabs, thick Arab, they look so similar, they even conduct their business in a similar way, thick Arab, he does not speak my language,* the barman has a long and aquiline nose, his eyes are dark, his lips are red as if they have been tattooed, hennaed. Volker leans forward towards a bar stool, he pulls the bar stool back from the counter so that he can edge around it, he rests his backside on the bar stool, he does not sit, not yet, he will sit later. *Budweiser, please, I can speak your language magniloquence, but you despise me, I am German, I speak French with a German accent, I think that all Greeks are feckless, I do not know why you despise me, or do you despise everyone, anyone who is not French, but you are not French, you are of North African descent, there has always been rancour between us, we are never satisfied with the cadences of our languages, communication is impossible so, therefore, we cannot co-exist.*

Budweiser, I drink American because I believe in a dream. The man behind the bar, who is possibly Moroccan or Algerian, certainly of a more Semitic extraction than an African one, *we are condemned because we do not speak the same language, you are a delinquent,* leans close to him, what? The music from the jukebox suddenly stops and there is a silence, not silence for there is sound, the sound of people talking to each other, *in words that they do not understand,* but silent of music. Volker looks out and across the tables, *I despise that song, there were times when I could imagine pain, it's been so lonely without you here, I'm like a bird without a song, now I know the pettiness of that passion that art paints so large, this sincerity, these words, nothing can stop this lonely rain from falling tell me baby, where did I go wrong, they tell me nothing, sincerity is an easy way to deny complexity, it is so undemanding.* The man with the pink swastika tattooed on his skull walks up to the machine and inserts a coin into it, he returns to the table where he was sitting, and then the music begins again. Budweiser, please. The man with the words Princeton Alumni on his T-shirt has moved, he no longer comforts the man who is in despair, maybe he became bored, *a sad story is always boring,* or maybe he just had an aeroplane to catch and so had to go. The sound that comes from the jukebox is the same sound, the same song, *melancholy, love has left me, I have left her, as her love has left, so has her memory. I have the memory but in time she who tortures me will no longer exist, twice, thrice, love is leaving me, it will soon no longer be here, it is not here, listen.* Volker looks at the man who put money into the jukebox, his hairless chest, *an ordinary face, so ordinary that it is familiar as there are so many ordinary faces, procrustean, graceless dead monkeys.* Volker looks at the man again, he is crying, several large tears have already dripped from his chest and formed pools on the table, he sits down, he hides his eyes with his hands, despite the music which appears to have gotten louder Volker can hear the sobbing, *the sound of water emerging from a tap for what is the eye but a water egress, grief, a lost love, ears are an outlet for love, laughter is all around me, he is the past, only the past explains his tears, did he too have the same flaw that I did, an original flaw, which was to need? And did he too not resist this flaw. The past is an illusion of today, a single tearlet of blood on a cherry blossom, the past defines him, but his past, and my past how dramatic are they, what rating would you give to this performance?*

KLINT MUST TAKE the boy away. He cannot lose all that he has gained, he cannot lose his love. And so Klint du Toit takes his fourteen-year-old son, George, by the hand. We need to get out of here and we need to get out of here fast. We can get into the car and drive away, to the airport. We can fly far away. We must go before I kill myself.

He sits behind the steering wheel of the Volkswagen Jetta. All four lanes of the highway are filled with traffic. He is caught between a red car – this is in front of him – and a blue car – this is behind him. His car is white. The windows are open because it is hot, the air is humid. Sweat drops from his face and gathers around his collar.

Turn on the radio. What has happened to cause this back-up? There must have been an accident, a person dying. I will die if we don't get moving soon.

If you are travelling on the A12 the off-ramp to the B6 has been closed due to a collision between two fuel trucks. There are several casualties, bodies are strewn across the road. There is a fire making its way across the motorway, following the line of fuel. If it jumps the tarmac it will spread to houses in the suburbs that are close by. Wind up your windows. Should you be driving in the direction of W take the Old Road off-ramp. This is a single carriage-way, built before the autobahn; it is not in good condition so proceed at a moderate speed. The cars on the off-ramp that has been closed will remain stationary for three to four hours. We stress at least four bodies have been placed in the road; it appears that there has not been time to cover them. Imagine that they are asleep.

Klint looks at his son, or the boy whom he says is his son. They have the same surname. One ray of sun that has emerged from behind the clouds bisects his face. He is impassive for he loves his father who is not his father but his uncle, his uncle who caresses him in the night under the stars in the dark bedroom. Klint takes an off-ramp into the suburb of Z, only then does he remember that the traffic lights in Z are not working; this may be because there has been a massive power cut in the whole of the area. It has lasted over four days. There have been reports that it was caused by an explosion at the generating plant but no one has been told whether this explosion was the work of a terrorist group or the result of a simple malfunctioning of the nuclear grid. It has been extremely hot. There have been reports of people frying eggs on the bonnets of cars and even one of an ominous cloud that gathered above a local fashion show. Many people thought it was the organisers who used a cloud to create a dream-like effect but others were more suspicious, particularly when it appeared that there was insufficient lighting to light the area, which became dark after the cloud appeared. Klint knows that workers are still attempting to locate all of the damage in order to repair the faults as this information is reported, on an almost hourly basis, on television and on the radio. They are working, always working. We Germans have the best workforce in the world. He also knows that there are still sporadic surges which have resulted in the traffic lights sometimes showing green when they should be showing red and sometimes showing red when they should be showing green. Collisions are always possible.

He touches his son, his nephew, his young friend, a slow caress. I will proceed with caution and treat all traffic lights as if they are four-way stops.

It is only midday and heavy pollution hangs above Z, smoke from the nuclear explosion, whether caused by

terrorists or not, has, as yet, not been blown away as there
is very little wind; or it may be global warming and carbon
emissions. But this is a first world country not somewhere
backward. It must be the refugees who set off the blast,
caused the malfunction, all those foreigners who are kept
in quarantined corrugated buildings on the outskirts of Z,
brown-skinned foreigners, sullen and sombre.

Klint rubs his hands across his shaven scalp and traces the
outline of a pink tattooed swastika in the stubble.

I must keep my lights on at all times and remain at a
lengthy following distance. He drives slowly past a school and
swears. There has been an accident. Two vehicles are blocking
the road. It would appear that the drivers did not realise that
the vehicles were too large to pass each other in the narrow
road, which has cars parked on either side of it. Any movement by either one of them will cause paint damage. Where to
now? Back to the motorway – there is an off-ramp … Maybe
we have avoided the collision and can get to the airport
quickly now. The plane leaves in three hours.

Klint du Toit sits behind the steering wheel of the Volkswagen Jetta. All four lanes of the highway are filled with
traffic. He is caught between a red car – this is in front of him
– and a blue car – this is behind him. His car is white. The
windows are open because it is hot. The air is humid, sweat
drops from his face and gathers around his collar. Déjà vu. He
imagines what it will be like to fly. He turns to his son who
is not his son. Imagine being in an airport. We will fly away.
Hold my hand, hold it tight, I love you, your soft skin, your
hard little cock. I will read to you all night, stories that you
love. I will stroke you all night, play with your beautiful body,
make you gasp with happiness.

VOLKER YAWNS, HE still has a long time to wait. *Shall I stay
here or shall I move on, I hate this song, it reminds me of my
memories, memories cannot be remembered.* He reaches into

his pocket, the same pocket of his trousers that he reached into when he approached the vending machine and then changed his mind. He leans forward, his face is close to the barman's now, *scared black hair on a chin, scarred, pockmarks, a maculation.* Budweiser, please. The barman nods and reaches below him. The door of the fridge opens, the barman takes out a bottle of Budweiser and, using the bottle-opener that hangs on a piece of string around his neck, opens the bottle. He throws the bottle-top into a nearby dustbin, the dustbin is underneath the bar counter, it is not visible, the barman does not speak as he hands Volker the bottle. He feels in his pocket and takes out a banknote; he hands it to the barman and nods. He glances at the man who still cries, his tears continue unabated, *he is an idiot.* The song on the jukebox comes to an end. Volker smokes a cigarette and drinks the Budweiser then he smokes another cigarette. Then he gets up and leaves the bar. He walks across the food hall, the heat is unbearable, he can feel the sweat as it drops down from his armpits, he licks his lips and tastes the salt of the sweat that gathers on his face, the salt of peanuts for in the bar he ate from the peanut bowl that was on the counter, he tastes salt and licks it from his lips, *salt from the ocean, salt crystals, salt from a body, pearls, undrinkable, bitter, thirsty, the ocean is before me, I sit and watch the sun set for the west is where the ocean is, western waters, bitter salt, cut skin on the background of a holistic new age, mutilation, the lines of salt crystals make up the ersatz necklace, kill me in your ocean of tears.* The parka hangs over his arm, the red jersey with the crew-neck reaches up to his chin. In Terminal 1 the heating system operates always. The heat is unbearable. He stops for a minute, places the suitcase that he's been dragging behind him between his legs, he hugs it with his thighs, he is a cautious man, he does not want anyone to take it from him and he knows that in large airports travellers are often preyed upon by thieves, pickpockets, *I am not credulous about human goodness,* it is easy to steal the bag of a passenger, *there is no human merit or sincerity, soon we will all die,* particularly one who has a lot of bags so that when he moves onwards he does not notice whether he carries, *drags across the concrete,* one or two of them, also many travellers are exhausted and lie down on one of the plastic airport chairs, these travellers do not have the luxury of the beds in the Business Class lounge, they must be content with the plastic chairs in the Economy airport halls, the plastic chairs that stick to their backs if they lie on them for a long time for the heating is hot, it is always constant and always turned up high, the heating heats for 24 hours and then another 24 hours and then another. It is effortless to remove a bag from a sleeping person even if it is underneath a head. They will not notice the movement if the bag is taken from them slowly and cautiously for they will be in too deep a sleep, dreaming, *there are only dreams, there is only the illusion of the dream, if there is no illusion where is the meaning,* exhausted from travelling so far, exhausted from being in Terminal 1, or from moving from Terminal 1 to Terminal 2C, *dead, stealing from the dead, we laugh at this tragedy for how else will we endure it,* which is where he will have to go in some hours. He stands still, he does not walk, he scans the rows of chairs, *the thieves that trail me, trail us, watching, waiting, planning, how I can sleep, I am an ant man, I am not a miniature man, a ghostly dumb goblin, a dwarf.* The suitcase between his legs is clamped firmly; *feel my knees against the hard outer carapace, kneel, bow to the god of these small things, the god of the universe is for sale, I can pay for it, gods cannot be stolen they can only be bought.* Volker puts the computer case on top of the suitcase so as not to have to hold it as he takes his red crew-necked jersey off, for a moment, as he wrestles the jersey over his head he is unable to see, as he is unable to see he clasps the bag more firmly between his thighs, for a moment, an imperceptible moment, he stops pulling the red crew-necked jersey over his head, the hard suitcase thrusts into his thigh as he lowers his body and leans forward, *a hand caressing me, hard fingers, stop, long fingers pinch my skin, soft, curling hard, the tight pull of hair caught in a zip*, then he removes the red jersey and his thighs relax, *infidelity, mine or yours, fidelity is a social construction, how can we be faithful, but infidelity is a more significant act of faithlessness for the adulterer always adulterates the truth, betrayal, it fills me with excitement, thirty pieces of silver, the garden at Gethsemane, even the soldiers recoiled in horror.* Underneath the red jersey he wears a T-shirt, it is white, there is a wet stain underneath his arms, it is visible as he reaches out to take the suitcase handle and then it is gone, clamped between upper arm and shoulder. Volker hesitates, then he continues to walk again, *where is that vacant chair*, the red jersey and the green parka remain draped over his arms, one item of clothing over each arm, he stops and puts the red jersey across his shoulders and now only the parka remains slung across his arm. A vacant plastic chair is not very far away, he only has to walk a few metres to get to it. He picks up the computer bag and takes hold of the handle of the suitcase, he walks with a purpose towards the chair, he has a purpose, he wants to sit down, he is tired and he wants to sleep, *a chair, a beautiful plastic chair, beauty, the chair is beautiful, I can experience this chair, this beauty, but do I experience it wrongly, it is only a plastic chair, everything that has a purpose is ugly, beauty has no purpose, beauty is wrong, the chair is beautiful, it has a purpose. I want to sleep, to lie down, to close my eyes, only that which serves no end is beautiful, the chair is ugly, beauty, plastic, endless plastic chairs, purposeful, useful, horrid and foul, exquisite.* Opposite the vacant chair, on another chair, sits the silent child, the same child who touched him as he passed earlier, *silence, we cannot speak the secret.* The child does not read or play a computer game, the child stares into the distance, into the vacancy of the people-filled airport, *what does he see, does he see dead stars that do not exist, the dead stars whose light is trapped in time, the stars painted on the ceiling?* Next to the child, there is a seat between them, are two women, they also sit, the women are talking to each other; the child is alone, *he too is alone. Why does betrayal open up a new landscape, a sensual adventure, and the possibility of new betrayals? It must end for he remembers …*

DO NOT MOVE.

George is a child in years, but his wisdom is that of an old man. He cannot move, not a muscle for once there was a mishap, a slip of a blade, and he lost a green eye. This was horrible; he knows that he does not want it to happen again, even though his lifeless eye now makes for a good photograph.

Klint arranges George's body on the plinth, legs slightly apart. Now Klint moves his head, first to the right, then to the left. He arranges his face, the crown of his head parallel to the shelf, mouth cast down, his eyes are not visible, his hair grows long over his brow. He is unclothed. His pale skin is smooth, his small legs do not touch the floor, there is no movement, smooth, he appears to be shaven but he is not for he is too young to have hair around his genitals, there is nothing on his legs, his chest, his arms, nothing to obscure their shape.

George has no hair.

Klint walks over to him and with a soft paintbrush draws in a few delicate rosebuds of hair. It curls at the base of the stomach and between the thighs. The hair is smooth, soft. The hair walks up towards the stomach. As it grows up, it narrows and then stops, somewhere, just at the waistline, further.

George feels a hand, long fingers on his slim hard chest that has no hair, smooth, lines.

Klint adjusts George's legs, slightly. They are splayed. The uncircumcised cock can be seen. Then he turns back to the table behind him and takes a rose from a vase. He places the rose on the erect cock, the flower balancing easily on the projectile. George moves slightly, a flexing of muscles, and the rose slips forward as if to fall. Don't move. Klint ties a silken black cord around George's balls and twists it over the erect cock. He tightens it so that if anything should happen to deflate the cock it will still remain standing for the silk is tight. George trembles in delight. The knife. Klint takes a blade from the table and hands it to him. George makes a small cut on the skin of the cock, just at the base, lightly. A red drop burns in the intense photographic light. It is round, a jewel. At the end of the cock is another jewel, slightly moist, a bead of anticipation. The liquid oozes and embraces the rose.

George arranges his arms and places his hand behind his head, a just-awake pose. Just awake is when the cock rises, sunrise, the dreams of the night. He moves his arms and hands again. They hide his face completely now. They cover the face as if it is crying, but he is not sad for if he moves his fingers his mouth curves upwards, a smile. Klint walks backwards. No, the body is not straight, bent slightly forward, not so far forward so as to obscure the cock, just enough so that the spine is curved. Klint focuses the hard light on the soft body. Behind it the wall is white, exacting, nothing obscures the image. The eye stares at him as if he is nowhere.

There is a stain is on the wall, just above the head, an insect, squashed, only slightly noticeable. Klint walks backwards and focuses the camera. Click.

Volker sits down, the heat is unbearable, *I am already in the desert, the lights drum down, neon rays, gamma rays, swimming in an ocean of neutrons, protons, the nucleus of the atom.* On a pole in front of him is an advertisement for sunscreen, a man, pink and a woman, also pink, *this colour, this baby-faced colour, cochineal heals a hurt, is called white, white a euphemism for pink or is the colour of white a multicolour, concinnity, pink is inconcinnate,* they walk on a beach, *white is the colour of milk or fresh snow, innocent and unstained, unblemished and bright, upright and honest, free from guilt and bloodshed.* The sun shines on their windswept hair, the man holds the hand of the woman, *hetero-norms,* both the man and the woman smile, their teeth are white, not pink, *bleached, reliable and honest,* as they walk out of the picture. Many Europeans are not used to the sun, they come from cold climes, but in Africa, Africa there is sun, BEWARE: first heatstroke, then cancer, BEWARE: the body acclimatises quickly, the blood thickens, *angry words, problem, death, red, fever, always exercise caution, be vigilant,* BUY CND, the European does not have the correct skin colour, *he is not black,* for the heat of Africa, it is always necessary to wear sunscreen as the European does not have sufficient melatonin in the skin. Black people have much melatonin in their skin, hence their skin is black, *dirt, messy, without light, dark and illegal, disastrous and dismal,* this is why white people came from Europe and black people, *horrible, malignant and grotesque, unhappy and unlucky,* from Africa. Volker is German, his skin is pink, *is it wise to tell a man who has cancer of the carcinogenic effects of the sun, a cancerous world, sick, stick to the medication it will make you well disposed to the sun, jaunty,* and his hair is yellow, a grey-yellow beneath his red beret. He sits on the chair and reaches beneath his white T-shirt which is stained with his sweat under the armpits. There is a chain around his neck, on the chain is a key, the key for the suitcase, or padlock that is attached to the suitcase, it is an old suitcase, not one that has an inbuilt digital lock, the suitcase is padlocked *where the fuck is the key, I cannot find the key, an inconvenient truth, in fact this is not true, I can find the key, it is the key to the suitcase not the key to the door that I once had, now this key is gone.* Volker always keeps the key on the chain around his neck, and when the padlock is unlocked he hangs the padlock there too, it must just be locked. He removes the chain from around his neck by undoing the clasp, the chain can be removed if he lifts it over his head but as it is short it is more difficult to do this, it gets caught in his hair or across his forehead, so he prefers to undo the clasp and then the key slips easily off the chain, he does not even need to remove the chain completely he can just undo the clasp then re-clasp it again. He takes the key from the chain, it is a silver chain, a cheap silver chain, a convenience not a decoration, where the chain has been around his neck is a scarlet revolutionary eruption as the chain is small, tight, *O, the story of O, the story of beads missing from the rosary, I take pleasure in the anticipation of loss, a silver loss, thirty pieces of silver, why were the soldiers in the garden so horrified?* He unlocks the bag, he opens it, he folds the green parka, first in half and then in half again, it is not too thick, there is space in the bag, it can easily fit into it, he closes the bag and locks it. For a moment he hesitates, then he unlocks the bag again, opens it and takes out the book, the travel guide, the word NAMIBIA on the cover, and puts it on the chair next to him, then he once more closes the bag and locks it. He puts the key back onto the chain and re-clasps it, his neck aches with the scarlet stain, he puts the chain and the key that is attached to it under his white T-shirt, *sleep, I can dream that I am alive.* The computer bag is between his legs, he is still vigilant despite being seated for he believes that thieves take things from unsuspecting travellers, the ubiquitous uniformity of luggage; a computer, a mobile phone, *I want this technological necessity, I want to keep my photographs,*[36] *a still photograph is always a picture of the dead, I want to meet the dead in the photograph and all I meet is my failure to meet them again, time and time again, photographs of*

---

36. Photographs always have a message: the politician smiling as he looks at the four mangled bodies of dead terrorists; the man who smiles because he swindled all the old people of a whole town; a loved child who cries; a naked man playing with his uncircumcised penis; a mother who is now dead. The text is in the lighting, the angle of the camera, the lows and the highs, the expression on a face. The photograph tells a story, the story of the photographer. To photograph a person is to take away their power: you are my story.

time gone, irrefutable time gone, a blank page that awaits my face, my name, not a picture of what is, what was, a photograph of me, my day-mare, my reverie. He puts the book into the top pocket of the computer bag so that it will be easily accessible should he want to take it out later. The red jersey lies on the arm of the chair, despite the heat he feels the need to put it somewhere where it will not be stolen, or where he will not forget it, he puts it around his shoulders, *the wool binds, catch me, what am I waiting for, I am waiting for it to be too late, too late to catch the train, too late to call out to my love,* the pools of sweat under his arms grows, *this time is oppressive as it leads to nowhere, there is nothing worse than unstructured time, I can do nothing for I am waiting for something, some event, I must sleep, I can wait no longer, I wait as I am in love,* there is more salt water, the material of the T-shirt under his arms is wet, he puts his right hand under his left arm, he takes it away and licks his fingers, *salty, cheeks a-glitter with tears, the ocean,* then he takes the red jersey from his shoulders and puts it on top of the computer. He looks to the left and notices the child again, the child that is alone although not alone, *I want to go away, I want to run away to sea, I want to be the boy that runs away to sea, I want the same feeling of the boy who runs away to sea.* The two women continue to sit next to him and talk. Volker can only hear a little of what they say to each other, something about baggage storage and lockers, *she has the look of a fanatic, a fanatic who thinks that she is a leader and yet she has never gained the respect of a single person, are there valuables in the baggage storage locker, or a bomb, ordinary women travellers moving from one place to another, the perfect disguise, a child, a perfect child who plays with fire and detonators, what does not kill you makes you stronger, or it kills you.* The one further away from him is young, she has green hair, her hair, an unnatural colour, there is a grey-blonde line that runs down the centre of her head, *it makes a path, a travelling path, walking to a rainbow, how invisible I am in this crowd, chemical green, nature is man-made.* The woman wears it short, it covers her forehead but not her ears, it has a gel on, it gleams in the neon light, *a high flyer in a hierarchy that thrives on Icaruses, they will always plummet to die.* The woman to whom she is speaking, the one that is further away from him, is older, she is very fat, her stomach undulates as she raises her hands to make a point in a sentence, *wax wings that melt in the heat, the always constant heat of neither summer nor winter but of the airport,* but then she may not be older, these days it is impossible to tell age, many people look younger than they are, many people look older than they are, *years of boredom and child rearing and work have written a line across their foreheads, or across their mouths, or lips augmented with collagen, faces paralysed with nerve gas, youth etched on age, a corpse already made up by the mortician, the smell of a harle-quin and lassitude.* The older woman stands up, she wears jeans and a T-shirt, as she rises from her chair her enormous breasts fall onto her colossal stomach, *they must not feed her, they cannot feed her,* it is a uniform, blue jeans, ubiquitous, some jeans are more expensive than others, but they are generally not too dissimilar, *and for those of you who are burning to ask, yes it's Armani, mine is a label.* She takes the handle of her bag and pulls it out, she has tucked it away so that it does not protrude from beneath the chair and so cause an accident, she is concerned, caring, *even the fat care for others despite the space that they take up in the world.* She takes the bag and as she walks away she pulls it behind her. The woman with the green hair takes a magazine from her large handbag and turns the pages, *Marie Claire, Vogue, Elle,* from where he sits he can see coloured pictures, fashion pictures, *glamour, thin and comely, who can say why chiffon draped over exiguity is beautiful.* The child sits on the white plastic chair, he does not read, nor does he speak. Volker looks around him, the sea of people has dissipated, only a few people gather in the area, there must be a hiatus in flights coming in, they will come in again, he knows this, and then the area will fill up; again, more people moving onwards, or backwards. He looks at the child. He swivels his head around, *I am an owl, 360 degrees, I watch the child, the owl of Minerva*[37] *only flies at night and yet I cannot tell whether it is night or day, am I wise?* Behind him to the left, standing directly behind a pillar so that only his arms are visible, is a man, he is tall and thin, every few minutes he looks out from behind the pillar, his head darts out and then is quickly pulled back again. He is not young, he is shaven, he has no hair, *he has no silver hair, as hers is silver, silver is the pinnacle of beauty, it must fall this tear of silver,* he slouches. Volker looks at him, the man in the bar, the man who cried, but because he does not lower his head the pink swastika is not visible, *what song does he play now?* The man is no longer crying, he returns Volker's stare, *this is a socially maladjusted person, we call ourselves salubrious, where is the world's medication?* The child looks at the man too. The child is aware that the man is looking at him, or is he looking at Volker, at the computer bag that lies between his legs? Volker pretends that he has not noticed the man who lounges behind the pole, but he is aware that he is being watched, *why is he there, I do not know why I am here, do I think to ask, does he?* The child seems to know that he is watched so he gets up from the white chair. The woman with the green hair who reads a fashion magazine does not look up from her reading, *Coco Chanel, style does not always make a*

---

37. In Roman mythology an owl accompanies the goddess Minerva, the goddess of wisdom; and so, in Western thinking, the owl is associated with wisdom, erudition and perspicacity. (Conversely, in African thinking the owl is associated with bad luck, death and evil.) The German philosopher Georg Wilhelm Friedrich Hegel said 'The owl of Minerva spreads its wings only with the falling of the dusk' and 'The owl of Minerva takes its flight only when the shades of night are gathering'. By this he meant that philosophy comes to understand a historical condition just as it passes, or flies, away. Philosophy appears only in the maturity of reality because it is only understood in hindsight.

fascist, the concatenation of the initials is the picture, the image of me, and the captions underneath them, take up her concentration. The child walks towards the man who slouches behind the pillar, he reaches out and touches the man's arm, *touch me for I want to learn your trade, your skill, I want to steal time, my time, the time that it takes to cross the floor, I want to be a time masturbator for only then will I despise it, the semen that is left in pools on the floor, I love the waste of human life, the taste of the waste, I enjoy the time that I spend with you, touch me as I touch you.* The man behind the pole does nothing, he does not look down at the outstretched hand, he barely moves, only his chest, concave then convex, as the air moves down into his lungs, *airways are freer.* The woman continues to page through the magazine, *she turns the pages so quickly, does she read the text, look at the pictures?* She has not noticed that the child is no longer next to her, possibly the child is not associated with her and she has no need to know where he might be for she does not care, she does not need to care about a lonely child who is not with her, although he appears to be, and yet he appears to also be lonely, alone, *I do not feel lonely, feeling lonely assumes a memory of not being alone and I have no such memory, my memory is the structure of time, I know how exact segments of my time are consumed.* Volker looks again at the man behind the pole, now he has lowered his head and Volker can see the pink swastika, *this is my shame, I am always reminded of it, no it is not a swastika it is an Asian sign.* The child now holds the man's left hand in his right hand, with his left the child takes something from the man, he holds it out to him with the hand that is free, the right hand, *I do not believe in sincerity,* a book, a package? Volker cannot be sure what it is. The man behind the pole still does not wear a shirt, his chest is bare, his black trousers are styled, every crease is in the correct place, *oh, my time is pleasure, but my life is tinged with longing, I want to hold a child's hand, read the pages of the book that he holds, he holds it out to me.* It is hot, very hot inside Terminal 1, this is possibly why the man has taken his shirt off for it is unlikely that he will become cold. Volker looks at the man and the child again, the child has the package, Volker can see that it is a package now, it is wrapped in brown paper, held fast against his chest, close to the closed buttons of his striped shirt that is peppered in blood, then he takes his hand from the hand of the man and reaching out he strokes the man's bare chest. The child makes a sound, Volker can hear it above the people sounds of the airport, the loudspeakers announcing flights that come from somewhere, move to nowhere, *I am in the ecstasy of misery, I am a wretched man.* After some minutes of this perplexing activity, and the sight of the woman with the green hair who fails to do anything, the child returns to his seat. Volker looks at him, their eyes meet. The child has one immobile eye, it reflects the neon lights that are above him, the neon lights of the airport that are always turned on, *can I open men's eyes, can I open them and not tear them out,* the package is no longer in his hands, but there is a bulge in the top pocket of his shirt, Volker can see it, it thrusts out from the red blood-stained material, it is the paper package, the package wrapped in brown paper, it is empty of words. The child opens his mouth, mouths the words, I am George, then he gets up, he is restless, and walks to another of the white plastic chairs, only one of them is vacant, then he sits down, the child almost sits on top of Volker the chairs are so close together, and yet the child must have moved for this chair was never as close to him as it is now. The child takes the package from his shirt pocket, he opens it, there are a number of pages in it. Volker looks at the child turning the pages, he turns them one by one … *I would like to read what is written here, a detective story, the story of a crime, it has well-rounded, not fat, but thin characters who bemoan their thinness, the thinness of their description, their anorexic stereotype, I have made peace with the blankness of these pages.* The pages that the child holds are pure white; they do not have a mark on them that might be a word. The child leans over to Volker. The child looks at him and points to the white page that he holds in his hand. The child has green eyes, one is motionless, his eyes remain open, they do not blink, *are these eyes the eyes of a ghost, the ghost of love?* He must wait. Volker sits on the plastic chair, he rests, he cannot sleep, he realised this a while ago, he is tired, the chair is uncomfortable, he cannot lie down, there are no other chairs available for him to stretch out on. In addition to this he is afraid that should he close his eyes, even for a moment, someone will make an attempt to steal his belongings and this he cannot afford, he has very little money, but also he is travelling to a destination where he does not know what it is he will be able to buy there. He knows little about Namibia, about Africa, he knows that it has cities and department stores *and yet, I am afraid, always afraid, I fear that I travel far away from civilisation, to savagery for this is what happens to civilisations when they do not take the medicine prescribed to them from the UN, from the World Bank, from those of us who are the keepers of knowledge, in this knowledge resides our power, we must defend our lack of useless things, but I am going, I am going anyway because the lancinating malignity of her silver hair must leave my memory, in this invidious annoyance there is no room for sentiment, it is as final as adamant, it is indelible, immutable, a fact, facts are not always true, I must remember my home for I will never return.* He will not return to Germany, he knows this, he may return, but never for long, he may not even remember the details of his home, *I must protect myself from home, from others, from her with the silver hair, I must create a barrier, a barrier called indifference.* Volker looks around him as he wants to find a bathroom, his mother, *my mother's face, she is fat, stringy blonde hair, culpable* and his brother, *the boygirl in Berlin,* he may not wish to contact them, it is only for the sake of courtesy, for form, politeness, that he has their photographs, their addresses and telephone numbers, *details; addresses and telephone numbers, photographs, the world will make me suffer, the addresses, photographs, telephone numbers, I will create a memorial with these details, the creation of a memorial is one way of forgetting for then I will only remember the memorial, only this memorial.* He took down all the details and recorded them on a computer, the computer that he clasps between his calves now that he is seated, the computer is valuable, it should not be stolen, *but there is still a trace, a trace of her perfume, she cannot leave this permanency, but the trace that she makes is a trace that requires erasure, there are no photographs for she is already dead.* And his bag, in it are clothes and toiletries, he will need all of these things for the journey ahead, for of course at the moment he arrives at his destination he cannot only have the clothes that he wears. He takes the brochure that he picked up at the INFORMATION kiosk from the pocket of his jeans, he looks at it, *a city map, an airport city map;* there are roads to the terminals, *circular roads, pantiles of aggravation,* shops drawn in detail, *maps for the bored and the lonely who have nowhere to go and who wait and who wait, this interminable time.* The walkways and the navette, the electrical bus, routes are drawn on the brochure in different colours, walkways are blue and navette routes are red and green. He looks at the brochure of the airport more closely, the curio shop that he went into earlier is there, *where I stole, what did I steal, I no longer have it, a keyring, an authentic African keyring, I have no keys,* and there is the bar, he looks more closely at the brochure, *we try to stave off chaos by a rigorous application of detail and order.* He turns it over, *a regulation of the organisation of this space, of this time, of all its activity; I feel examined and inspected, a speck of blood under a microscope.* Terminal 2C is far away, he does not know how long it will take him to get there, not 5 hours, and he still has 5 hours to wait, but certainly the distance will not take him 5 minutes to traverse, an hour at least. Volker studies the map, *I have the intelligence of a vole, where do I go, this space is a vast emptiness built on emptiness, I am the master of wisdom, but no one knows what wisdom is?* He will have to go down at least 2 escalators, then take the navette 4 stops, this will probably take at least an hour, or at least 30 minutes, but he has to find the navette buses and then he does not know how long it will take for one to arrive, the brochure says that navettes arrive and depart every 15 minutes, will he arrive at the depot just as one is departing, in which case he will have to wait 15 minutes, or will he arrive just as one is about to depart, in which case he will wait no time at all. The navette will take him directly to Terminal 2C, but he will have to get off at the correct stop, Volker counts the stops on the brochure, there are at least six of them, they are well marked, *red on white*, it will be inconvenient if he gets off the navette at the incorrect stop, the one after the stop that he has to get off at, then have to retrace his path, walk to the other side of the navette station, get on another navette, back-track to the correct stop, or if he gets off the navette too early, then he will have to catch the next one, only one stop but he will have to wait for it, wait at least 15 minutes for the next one to arrive, and what happens if it is full, then he will have to wait another 15 minutes for the next one. The time that it will take him to get to Terminal 2C is not precise, the brochure is imprecise, it leaves much to planning and further planning, it leaves much to supposition, *what is the plan if there is no future, what is the future for the future is what I plan now, I must have certainty about the time it will take to get to Terminal 2C, I must know the space, absolute certainty for if I do not then I am lost, my theories are obsolete, but all of this is relative, the time it takes to arrive and depart, the time of the journey, I must let it go, I must let my plans go, but if they go then everything will go with them, I will have no illusion of control.* He looks more closely at the brochure, he holds it closer to his eyes, there are small pictures of small moving cars, parking spaces in Terminal 1, but there are no cars in the building, *are they grains of sand,* there are parking garages at the airport but these are not in the building itself, *grains of sand dammed by the flatness of the paper,* and yet there are spaces on the brochure that are clearly marked with small moving vehicles, they are drawn as if they are moving, *the images move, it is a matter of dimension, two dimensions not three, three not two, what is a one-dimensional thing, can we know of the tenth dimension?* He looks up from reading the brochure and notices that, in the distance, there is a moving vehicle. It is coming towards him, the signs on the pamphlet indicated these vehicles, these carts with engines attached to them, the engines are powered by electricity, as is the navette, *moving carts, golf carts.* These carts take passengers from one end of a Terminal to the navette bus station, *elderly, arthritic joints, I am so tired, I am no longer young, where is the youth of my yesterday, I do not feel like the long walk, and the young always defeat the old, the strong the weak, and there is nothing wrong for tomorrow the young will be the old, the weak will be the strong, the carts will carry the old today and the young tomorrow, it will make no difference whether I do one thing or another, whether I catch the cart or not.* Volker leans back in the chair, the woman with the green hair is no longer next to him, he did not notice her as she left her white plastic chair, she is paging through her magazine somewhere else, or she is not paging through it, he does not know, all he knows is that she has disappeared, possibly she has a navette to catch and thought it necessary that she leave. The child who seemed to be with her but now, he realises, was not, continues to sit on the chair next to him. The child is not her child, or a child that she knows, the child is not travelling with her, but then possibly she is at a nearby shop because she wants to buy something, some hand cream or perfume from the shop that is opposite Volker and the child, not directly opposite them, but slightly to the right, Volker does not have to move his head to see it, but if he does if becomes clearer, the sign outside of it reads Fine Perfumes, the picture on the billboard is of Kate Moss. *Where is Kate Moss in this airport?*[38] *Obsession, a liquid golden picture, does she walk with her luggage the same route that I will walk, will she walk next to me?* The woman may have gone to buy a beer or smoke a cigarette, and told the child to wait for her, to remain on the chair that he sits on, *fine perfumes disguise, they are clothing, I am clothed in a smell, the smell of coition, the smell of my indifferent difference.* The child looks at the white blank pages in front of him. Then he looks up, again, at the man who wears no shirt and who has a swastika tattooed to his skull and who still stands behind the pole. He has moved slightly so that only his left arm is visible. The child takes out a pen and begins to write, *black spirals on the page, he invents a truth, philosophy will clip angel's wings, un-weave a rainbow.* Volker feels uncomfortable, the computer bag is between his legs and the child sits too close to him. The child continues to write, but, between words, between concentration, turns to stare at him, *the owl of Minerva flies only at night, it spreads its wings when the light begins to fade, dusk, wisdom always takes flight at the end of the day, after everything has happened, I will only ever understand in hindsight.* Volker picks up the suitcase and the computer bag, then he places the suitcase in front of him and pulls the handle from the front top slot, he leans over and attaches the computer, or rather the computer bag, onto it,

---

38. In the cult novel *American Psycho* by Brett Easton Ellis there are repetitive, sometimes bordering on irritating, allusions to fashion and brand names; designer clothing, designer perfumes, designer cars, designer wines, even designer knives and razor blades. Every character is described with exact reference to the fashion brand he or she is wearing, driving, smells of; even if they are naked with a raging gerbil in a vagina or anus they will be wearing a Hermes scarf. People are a brand, a dilation of culture and an annihilation of reality.

now he only has one bag to take care of, or rather one item. As he gets up from the chair the child moves closer to him, then the child leans forward and puts his hand out, he touches Volker's hand gently, *a whisper,* then he grasps Volker's hand, *I am dead, I am like a flame under glass, I flicker and then I will go out because there is no air, I am absurd for I am nothing but a word picture in a book, look at what I draw, it is me.* Volker stands upright, he takes the child's hand from his own, *I cannot, I cannot,* and begins to walk away. He pulls the suitcase and the computer that is on top of it along behind him. The child raises his head from the blank page that is filled with black spirals, *writing is not about something, it is the something itself,* he watches Volker as he gets up and leaves, *to make the choice to leave is a tragedy, why is he choosing to leave, can I make him choose something else, to stay, he will leave me, he has to leave something behind when he makes this choice, one always does. He will betray me as they all betray me, they all leave. I am the owl; it is twilight in this ever present neon.* The child waves to Volker as he walks away. There are three doors in front of him, he will have to walk past at least four rows of chairs and then across an open space if he wants to reach them. He wants to wash his face and his hands, travelling is dirty, *germs are everywhere, doorknobs, these sheets, your mouth, they all have been enswathed, touch me here,* he wants to freshen up after the flight, the flight from his home in Germany to Terminal 1, *all voyages are a fiction, and all the places I have passed dream on in my heart.* As he walks towards the three doors he searches for a sign. He looks at the three doors, the one on the right has a picture of a woman on it, it is the woman's bathroom, *all pageant is decoration, and each voyage to find her hair stays silver, a metaphysical manifestation in my inmost heart,* the one on the left has a picture of a man on it, this is the one that he will enter for he is a man, *my playhouse is the man, I know myself, the mystery of the world is the visible not the invisible, I am shallow, I reach for my manly performance, it is the theatrical.* But he does not walk towards it and push it open, instead he looks carefully at the door in the middle of the two doors that have a picture of a man and a woman on each of them, the door in the middle of them has no sign on it at all. It is a green door, whereas the other two doors are blue, there is no sign that says NO ENTRY, nor is there a picture that indicates that behind the door is something hazardous. He wants to enter the green door, *I want to find something that is mysterious,* and so he pushes at it and it opens. An older woman stands a metre inside the entrance of the square room, which is lit only by a powerful spotlight at the back of it. Behind her, towards the back of the room, is another woman, she is younger. Volker recognises them as the two women who were smoking in the bar. *Where am I? I want to capture you for I am tired for want of nothing else to do, I must catch that right thing now, where are you?* The older woman who stands at the back of the room has removed the white smock with the green writing above her right breast, she is now dressed in a short purple dress; it rises up over her knees and stops where her groin begins. She wears black stockings, they have several holes in them, at least two on the right leg above the knee and one on the left leg on the thigh, the suspenders for each are clearly visible. The purple dress is short, so short that Volker can see that she wears no underwear. She stands in front of the powerful light, now it seems to light up the whole room, and, as the light is behind her, her dress is transparent; he looks at her body and stares at her unclad crotch, *don't pick fights with angels, they fight dirty,* she does not answer, but bends over, her back is to the wall, and picks up the broom that lies at her feet. As she bends over and picks up the broom he notices her skin, it is freckled, age spots, *and the young defeat the old, what I have is for free, I will give it to you, free as a gift for I have nothing to give, I have patience, I am indifferent to delay,* the skin hangs from the underside of her arms, it swings as she moves to pick up the broom, the skin on her legs is pale, what is visible above the elastic of the suspenders on her legs is slack. She turns around, her hair is brushed back and fastened into a tight bun, he notices that a few strands of it have escaped the pins that hold it. As she bends over, he looks again and notices her cunt, it is surprisingly firm and pink for one who is so old. The young woman who stands closer to the door watches him watch her, she also wears a purple dress but this one is long and falls to the ground, her face is covered by a white scarf, she is dressed as a nun would dress, there is a crucifix hanging from a chain that is around her neck, *tighter, tighter, Jesus must die, he thrashes in pain, the pain of his broken limbs*, the eyes that looked at him are green, she does not stand against the light so her dress is opaque. This is the cleaners' room, here there is everything that a cleaner needs; a broom, a mop, floor polish, some rags, *are you here as you have a complaint, is this why you came in here, is everything not to your satisfaction? I work night and day, every day the same day, every day the same night.* Volker looks at the older woman, *she is getting older, her brow wrinkled, her hair thinner? The alive are slow, the alive are dead,* her earrings hang down to her shoulders. Suddenly the old woman lifts her dress a fraction, it cannot be more than a millimetre, she only has to lift it slightly as it is very short, she thrusts her pussy at him and waits, *describe yourself in a single sentence, I am a very modern man, I fornicate and I read the paper.* Volker does not speak, *do you want me* he turns to the younger woman, the nun, *I can only believe, I am not eternal, I have lost the illusion that I will be eternal and so I have no meaning, I believe as I have no meaning, my belief means much to me, those were your words, I have no heaven and so I believe, but you do not want a believer, you want a pussy, there, take hers, for I am unable to give you what I believe in, I believe the pussy of the Virgin Mary is forever closed. To fuck you will be to kill you …*

THIS ROOM IS a den of pornography, a cleaning room where no one goes for no one cleans anymore. To live is a dirty business, dull with the dust of remembering.

The room – it is a large room – is used to store the cleaning agents needed by the cleaners. Maria, a fifty-something Bulgarian supervisor, has the key. She collects the buckets and the rags and the various poisons early in the morning and returns them late at night. Maria is the gate-keeper to this hideout of pornography. What comes out; videos, movies, photographs, everything digital, images for those who travel in another world besides the one that they are living in. Fantasies. This is art. Maria works for the cleaning company Nous Nettoyons les Toilettes du Monde or We Clean the World's Toilets.[39] This is just a part-time job. It creates a foil for a respectable working-class woman. Actually Maria is an artist disguised as a worker. She performs for the world; she is the granite on which dreams of a better society are built. She is art. She enjoys this part, this haloed hallowed role. It sanctifies her, sharpens her awareness of her abjectivity, as a woman, as a worker. It is a position, a position of poison.

Her co-worker, or co-movie star, is Velda. She is twenty. Velda is not self-aware, although she takes many selfies; she just needs the cash. They are in this room because Dick – who is slim and always wears clothes that have a very conspicuous label on them; today he is wearing the Gucci belt he bought from the flea market in Saint-Germain-des-Prés, a fake Gucci belt – is a director, an auteur of the sublime. I Love Dick, says Maria; I love Dick, says Velda. Dick likes to use this room for it is a secret room in a public place, a secret that is forever not

39. The company, We Clean the World's Toilets, is an American company, and as Google is also an American company, it is patriotic to use Google Translate to translate the name of the company into all the world's languages, for even Americans can recognise that not everyone speaks American. In France it is translated into French.

a secret but is never revealed. He is halfway through making a movie on the power of the machine: how machines fuck men and women, exhilarate them, how they can make you fly, high. Dick is not merely a pornographer. He, like Maria, is an artist. When he is not in this room making this movie he is a performance artist. He performs in public places – Paris, New York and Los Angeles, inside and outside opera houses, shopping malls, museums and galleries. He also, although he has no permission to do so and is always on the lookout for a policeman, does performance art in this airport. But he is satisfied for often a distraught bored passenger will come across his art and smile, or scream, it alleviates boredom. His body is his art, a photograph. He decorates it, travels to it, uses his body, his muscles to convey an idea forward, to make us think that, just for a moment, we are not tourists trapped in the life of others, but people trapped only in our bodies. And we can never escape the body. We can only make it fly. We do not need feathers for, like Dick, we can direct the birds.

Dick likes Maria. He likes older women. They are wise, unlike those twenty-something floozies who come to his performances. And Maria, she has read the work of Marinetti.[40] She believes in the art of the movie maker, the director, the power of machinery to make art, to be art. In this movie she is a machine. In the last one she was a Mexican refugee, starving. She crossed the border to save her five children, fleeing from a drug lord who, while providing

40. Filippo Tommaso Marinetti, an Italian, developed an ideology in which he set out the worship of the machine. Our hearts were filled with an immense pride at feeling ourselves standing quite alone, like lighthouses or like the sentinels in an outpost, facing the army of enemy stars encamped in their celestial bivouacs. Alone with the engineers in the infernal stoke holes of great ships, alone with the black spirits which rage in the belly of rogue locomotives, alone with the drunkards beating their wings against the walls. Should you want to explore this philosophy further, read the *Futurist Manifesto* which starts with the words 'And we hate sentiment, it is real' and ends with 'We wish to glorify war, it is the sole cleanser of the world.'

her children with medical care and schooling, also had a penchant for heroin and violence. Maria is an eclectic star. She performs for Dick and herself. She fashions her power in terms of her abjectness, her wretched self-effacing place in the structure that surrounds her; her command lies in her bitterness. She is powerful. She worships power. She is the moving photograph.

Dick likes Maria. She sucks his cock better than any person ever has, and he has had his cock sucked many times; she sucks it as a sublime machine would do. She is a machine, a man-made machine which, like Hal in *2001: Space Odyssey*, is out of control.

Dick is a skilled director. In his movies one shot is placed in quick succession with another. The cut and thrust of the images create a visionary rumble, a cacophony of steely sounds. Wooden mannequins face the sun, lighted darkness, they are a conveyer belt of sex and thunder, the bodies the screws that hold the nuts. He records foreign-sounding voice-overs, Russian, menacing, electric, liquid, metal clashing with skin; there is iron in the soul and against the wind. And Maria is the wind and the stars and the faded, aged glamour. She catches her shame in a net woven by spider-shaped fingers. The humiliation that she knows is always there; she makes an aura of her image, her simulated image, her performative twin. She lifts her skirt high and shows the white teeth that line her cunt, her skin is dappled with the cellulite of years of anorexia. Her body is the limitless sky.

Velda is an extra in the movie. She was employed just for the day. She plays the nun to Maria's time-machine, the nun who sees God in the mirror. God in a cunt, God everywhere for God is good, God is a powerful elixir, God embraces the self as Velda could never embrace herself, as only Maria can embrace herself.

And Dick, he likes to make movies in this space. It is cheap. He rents it from Maria. Nous Nettoyons les Toilettes du Monde, or We Clean the World's Toilets, is unaware that Maria does this. They are unaware that the room is used most nights and almost most days as a room of perversity and art, a room where ideas are sabotaged, texts undermined and scripts rewritten. Dick knows that Maria earns a lot of extra money from him, but he is unconcerned because this is destabilisation. He is emasculating a society in which he is entirely male. He is part of the sub-culture of sabotage. He disrupts as many systems as he is able, and together with Maria – he could not do it without her – they are the talk of the art world.

Art, like God, is fabulous and famous for as long as it is believed in. Maria urges Dick to make simple movies, just one fuck and then shots, quick shots of amputated, deracinated limbs that reach out to nowhere, nothing complicated or sincere, no emotion. And in this denial of sincerity, so here lays the complex, the skeleton is laid bare, open as a cunt is open, stripped of all meaning, something that is just there. There are no secrets; the greatest secret in the world is that there is no secret. A secret is never just under the overcoat.

And Dick, Dick loves Maria, not only because he has never experienced such amazing blow jobs, but also, unlike her, he knows or does not know, that he has a need to anchor himself to someone, someone to keep him from falling. Maria knows this, but also knows that a boat adrift on the ocean is not powerful. She does not like the idea of motherhood. And she prefers to blow Jean Claude, that little golden brown thief who looks like an angel.

The movie is as yet incomplete. When it is finished – and this will be in about four months – it will be shown at the California Art Center in Los Angeles, and thereafter in Miami, Prague, Venice and Buenos Aires. Already the art circuit waits breathlessly. There is an air of anticipation: Dick and Maria, Dick and Maria. Hail Art; and Velda.[41] And Maria thinks that

41. The movie was later to win the following awards:
   Las Vegas Film Critics Award

this time she will go to Los Angeles, and she could ask Jean Claude to accompany her. Yes, this may be a whole lot of fun. They could run down the boulevard of broken dreams. She will be an Eastern European Elizabeth Taylor and Jean Claude a brown James Dean.

VOLKER TURNS RED, he blushes, and opens the door that leads out into Terminal 1. The blue door to his right, whereas previously it was to his left, is marked with a picture of a man, the universal male, the man does not wear a dress, *it is a universal symbol as it is not a universal symbol, there are no words, it is a language that is not understood, make a mistake and you enter the wrong room.* Volker looks at the picture on the door *why had he made a mistake? All germs are disguised.* The etiolated women, *always everywhere,* mop and sweep and vacuum, *at night, a lady of the night, I am open 24 hours and then another 24 and then another 24, I am always full, I glide past you as a ghost will glide, through walls, into closed rooms and cupboards, it is always full in this airport, there is never a time when it is empty. I am a hiatus, there are always people, take my pussy and stroke it.* He stands next to the door to the men's toilet, it swings open, he must have stepped on a button that is in the floor for he did not touch the door, he did not push it open. Volker walks inside, at the washbasin he turns on the cold tap, water rushes out of it, he cups both his hands under the water and then scoops it up, he throws it over his face, the water is cold on his face, it is a respite from the heat of Terminal 1. He does this again and then a third time, *but I did want her, I wanted to take her as she stood there, I want to fuck her till she screams, what a fantasy, what a story, there is no end to this fantasy, she is a blankness, a hole in the grain of*

Globes de Cristal Award, France
National Film Award, Bangladesh

things, and one fantasy can fill this hole as well as any other.
He looks into the mirror that is above the washbasin; there
is a mole just underneath his left eye, only in the mirror it is
underneath his right eye, *am I looking at a replica of myself,
a real fake.* A man stands next to him, slightly to his left, if
Volker moved one step closer to him he could touch him,
Volker makes himself look at the mirror, he will not look
sideways …

Wallace looks into the mirror. He is irritated and annoyed
that he has to be in this Terminal, Terminal 1, but he had to
meet a client here. Now he has to get all the way to Terminal 2 where he must oversee a transaction, ensure that all will
go well, although he knows that it will for he has been – he
always is – meticulous in his preparation. And he is irritated
because the client he has just met with was fussy and choosy:
the child must have emerald green eyes and chestnut hair
and have no Russian blood whatsoever – as if anyone could
tell what type of blood a person has. Wallace looks into the
mirror, but all the mirror does is look back at him. Someone
looks at him as he looks into the mirror, someone on his left,
and yet the mirror does not seem to look at him, instead he
looks at the mirror. He is a self-reflexive pronoun. How self-
reflecting is a mirror? A mirror is instinctive, a picture of the
real, a portrait of the self, a portrait of the artist as a young
man, the desert of the real, a repetition, a plagiarism, a dop-
pelganger. Who is in the mirror? Can it be he?
    Wallace wonders what he is doing in this airport – in a
metaphorical sense because he knows why he is here. He
often wonders why he does this work, when he could be an
actor, a performance artist. He has always been praised for
his ability to mimic others, to play a role. He remembers how
his mother praised him as a young boy. He played the role of
the boy king in Richard III. And yet he knows that he is there
for a purpose. Some would say an unethical purpose; others

would say a man has got to eat. Sometimes he thinks that he should change his profession. He is bored. But then he also knows that he has few marketable skills and so should remain doing what he does best.

Wallace looks at the mirror and the mirror looks at him, at the body which for him is his city, his all, his dwelling place, his only domain. He only has himself, he cares for only himself.

Will the child live in a city, or will he take him far away, somewhere in the provinces where he will be safe from the sounds of the traffic, safe from the prying eyes of the camera on the corner?

Wallace has a lot to think about.

The lines on the forehead are a road, and so he looks at the roads. There are four of them, straight roads, parallel roads. They go down, nowhere, they start somewhere up. They start somewhere and they go nowhere. They start on the right and they start on the left, end right start left, start left, end right. Strands of hair hang over his forehead. The strands hang over the lines that are roads, hair bisects the roads, hair is an alley, many alleys lead from his crown down to the roads, grey alleys that move upwards, lead into a forest, a forest of many more alleys, and in the alleys are people, thin grey people clustered together, the alley people go somewhere, else. The city of the mirror has two holes, pools of blue water, a fresh-water lake, a slime dam, a chlorinated swimming pool. His eyes shine, tears, the mirror cries, highlights the chlorinated waters.

Wallace often wonders if he is a poet as well as a trader.

A hill is in the middle of his face, there are two holes in it, these holes breathe, air enters the city by way of these holes, holes that enter the round city structure and descend down to its inner workings, here are his lungs, lungs of progress, for in a hill somewhere someone may find gold, gold is sustenance, sustenance for city objects, city people, blue chlorinated waters. His red lips open and close, his lips are bitten by white teeth, covered in flecks of blood, nourishing chlorinated white blood cells, they are his immunity, white teeth bite, bite wide thighs, white teeth extinguish, a woman on a bed, white teeth are fluorinated dental structures.

He sighs, and thinks that the metaphor of a city is the best metaphor he can imagine to describe his face. He looks into the city and the traffic that is on the roads, he looks into the city and the hills. The hills vibrate, they breathe, have life. He looks into the city and leans forward to bite at it. The city is nourishing, exciting, stimulating, he bites the mirror, bites at the roads that go nowhere, the hills that may hold value and the water that is chlorinated.

Wallace looks at the ducks that swim on the blue chlorinated water and then, as he looks more closely, they die, poisoned by shards of mirrored glass.

Is this what he is, a poisoner?

And who is the man that stands to his left?

VOLKER LOOKS AT the man, he does not want to, he does not want to do anything that may make the man think that he is in any way interested in him except as someone he has bumped into in the restroom for he, too, is a travelling man, so he looks at him in the mirror that is in front of him. *I look into the mirror and the mirror looks back at me, at him,* and yet the mirror does not look at him, he looks at the mirror, *the mirror looks at him, I am a self-reflexive pronoun, but how self-reflecting is a mirror, a mirror is instinctive, it is a picture of the real, a portrait of the self.* He looks at the man in the reflection, the man that stands next to him, he looks at the strands of hair that hang over the forehead, over the lines on his forehead. The man stands to his right. Volker turns on the cold tap, the water rushes out if it, he scoops it up and then he throws it over his face, the man who is next to him repeats these gestures, he is following him, *consistency is the gremlin of a little mind, copy me, make me small, smaller, a mirror image*, but the mirror is not in front of him, it is to his right, and yet there is a mirror in front of him, he cups more of the water and splashes his face, his face in the mirror does the same thing, the man to his right does the same thing, *a meniscus with an strange mark on the forehead, dirt, a laceration, let me wash away this mark, I am a mirage, what is my face, where is the knife that wounds me.* Volker takes a handkerchief from his pocket, a freshly folded bed of cotton, he wipes the cold water from his face, *water, the drops of dreams,* he wipes down his face for he cannot use the heating fan that blows warm air onto the wet skin of newly washed hands, the heating fan is not angled so that it will point at a wet face, his face is cool. The man to his right moves slightly, he leans towards Volker, *he moves, the mark changes places, across the left eye, there is no eye to stare at, a shadow cast by his stretched out arm, the satyr, an incubus that sucks the soul from water,* also wipes his face, although he does not take a handkerchief from his own pocket instead he takes Volker's, *thank you very much, thank you very much, we are all mechanical dolls, turn on the switch and I will do what you want me to do, I have been around the world often, several times, it is desuetude that interests me, I seek it like a heat-seeking missile with the relentlessness of the hunted, thank you I bow to you for I have found you again, found the predictable in you, I seek the commonplace, my cheeks glitter with the tears of my gratitude.* The man wears a white T-shirt, it looks remarkably similar to Volker's own shirt, *pallid as a rainbow, I am indifferent to him, he is not me, I cannot be indifferent to me, he is not me, he is already moving towards the periphery of my imagination.* Volker now feels the need to urinate, he did not have this urge a moment ago as he splashed down his face, but now he does, *running water, an oasis of horror.* Behind him and to his left are several urinals, they are public and he does not want to urinate publicly, he does not want to expose himself to this man who only a moment ago stood next to him and splashed water on his face, in the same way that he splashed water on his face, as if he was him, a mirror image. Volker looks around the bathroom; there is a brown door against the wall behind him, a stall in which there will be a toilet. He turns around and walks into the stall, and then he closes the door behind him. On the wall in front of him are the words: more than 7 inches, meet me here before the 10pm flight to Alabama, I like to suck and fuck. He looks into the toilet bowl, he leans over and lifts the half lid from it, the ashen bowl is soiled, *is this the reflection of my newly cleaned face, I am Dante's guide, why did you leave me only faeces, smear it across the white mirror of the bowl, across my face, my colour is brown, faeces in the morning,* it is as if the women who clean the airport restrooms have never been into this toilet stall to clean the toilet bowl, or possibly they have but as there is only one toilet in the men's bathroom it must be used regularly and maybe the women cleaned it much earlier, *it just gets dirty again, very quickly, the promise of leaning into the white bowl that is brown, how flat are promises, they always hold me back, they are never delivered.* On the other hand it is possible that the women who clean in Terminal 1 do not come into the men's bathroom and that the task of cleaning out the toilet is that of a man, and Volker has not noticed any male cleaners in Terminal 1 so they must come to clean irregularly. He urinates, a long stream of yellow liquid falls into the water at the bottom of the toilet bowl. He flushes the toilet and turns to leave the toilet stall. He walks back into the bathroom, there is no longer anyone there, he is alone, *alone with only the image of myself in the mirror, find a mirror and shake it, shake out the image, hold it up and stretch it out like licked wet skin.* He walks over to the washstands and turns on the tap, once again he feels the cold water pour onto and over his hands. He looks up at himself, he is tired. Volker leaves the men's bathroom, *the imbroglio of a putrescent toilet, shattered,* he walks with a hesitant gait, it appears as if he is uncertain as to where he wants to go to, *make time go faster, waiting time will always go slowly, unstructured shapeless time is vexatious, the appearance of time speeding, make the time go faster, make me feel old so that a year is only a percentage of life.* He knows that sleep will make time pass quickly, *night, asleep in a bed, at home, a hotel, an airport hotel wide open flesh between hot thighs, the flight of a bird moving against a cloud, wanton reckless flight, the moment of sleep, the moment of wakefulness, the hands on the clock are always in the same place, an indication of time gone by, the morning is always brighter.* But he cannot sleep in Terminal 1 for he is afraid, afraid that while he sleeps someone, some thief, will steal his bags, his bag of clothing and his computer. He walks back to the chairs where he sat previously, where he sat next to the young boy. He looks around him, the boy is no longer there, he has moved off to somewhere else, *I have a desire to hold onto the boy, I want to hold him,* or possibly he has joined the woman with the green hair, the one who was reading a magazine whom he assumed was the boy's mother, or he has joined the man with the pink swastika tattooed onto his shaved head, the boy's guardian, his guardian if only for a brief period, *hold me, I desire you, let me enjoy you, the desire to hold and desire to enjoy are mutually destructive, I will not destroy you, I want to hold you.* The boy is not where he was previously so now the chair on which he sat is vacated, empty. Volker walks quickly towards it for he would like to put his feet on it, at least stretch out. He reaches the chairs and sits down, he moves the chair that is next to his, the one on which the boy previously sat, in front of him, there is a red mark on the white plastic seat, *another single tearlet of blood.* He puts his bags under the chair, the computer bag is still on the top of his other bag, it is still attached to it, *I travel with only one object, I am modest, I understand how small my space is.* He leans down, the chair on which he sits leans against a wall. He unlocks his suitcase, opens it and takes out the green parka, he places it on top of the bags, *cover them over, disguise them, pretend that I have nothing to steal, I will not sleep, but in case, just in case, nothing visible for the eye of a thief, a rolled up dirty old green parka.* The parka is not old and not dirty, however, in the way that he has placed it and from a distance it looks old and dirty. He leans his head back against the wall. The wall is hard so he takes the red jersey that is still around his neck, it is hot in Terminal 1, *feel the sweat drip, water runs fast why can't time, diamonds of sweat, diamond dogs bark loudly, so hot,* from his shoulders, *relief,* it feels cooler, *no burning around my throat, a small animal has been murdered, removed, a small animal strangles me, a white neck exposes my body temperature.* He arranges the red jersey underneath his head, he places it against the wall so that as he leans backwards his head comes into contact with it, the wall does not feel as hard as it did before, it is soft, *soft, hot soft, my head is filled with heat.* But at least the red jersey against the wall is soft; he leans his head backwards and closes his eyes. He knows that he will not sleep. There are a lot of voices around him, *once upon a time in Alaska there was a fountain that was a frozen fountain, merrily merrily merrily merrily life is but a dream, look closely at the roof, it is not a ceiling, it is concrete, it is white, look closely and you will see the witches that ride in the grains of sandwiched sand, the economy is hurting, buy a house at a prime rate, follow the rats, they are racing along a car track, they are streaming into embankments, a rat race dammed by the waters of Lethe.* In front of him, opposite the chairs that are lined in rows is a television screen, he had not noticed it before, he was so eager to get a beer and have a cigarette, he focused on finding a place in which he could do this, or he was tired so that the thought of television did not come into his mind for he was intent on finding a chair, two chairs, one on which he could put his feet up, the second to sit on, or maybe it was not there then. Now, in front of him on the opposite wall the television flickers, people turn to face it, they watch the pictures, *human beings are retinal creatures, I need the light to breathe, this means nothing to a bat, a bat is disturbed by the sounds that materialise from the television, the frequencies jam its radar.* Volker sits up and looks at his watch. As he does so the red jersey that was behind his head, the one that he used to cushion his head against the hard white wall, falls to the ground. He leans over to pick it up, *what is the time, can I forget that time is essential to structure, check the time.* As he leans over to pick up the jersey he remembers that he does not know the time, not that the time is relevant, however he would like to know it, *I will never reach that point of ecstasy, the complete step across chronological time into timeless shadow, wonderment in the bleakness, the sensation of death kicking at my heels, a phantom trailing at death's heels, and me hurrying to a plank from which angels leap off and fly into the void of uncreated emptiness, magic moths in heaven.* Volker looks at his watch, it is 16h00, he sat down on the chair at 14h45, he looked at his watch minutes before he put his hand back and felt the hard wall behind it, then he took the jersey from his neck and folded it into a square, almost a cushion shape so as to make himself more comfortable, he slept for an hour, *and in sleep I hear a seething sound, not in my ear but everywhere, it has nothing to do with the echo of sound, the sound is not there when no one can hear it, I am dead and have been reborn numberless times but I cannot remember because the transition from life to death and back are ghostly, falling asleep and waking up again, the sound of waking, the sound of the normality principle, it bites like a spider bites.* He feels underneath the chair for his bags, the outline of the computer bag is rough beneath his hands, then the outline of the suitcase, they are both there, while he slept no one stole his luggage. He sits up, his face still shows a sign of recent sleep but on it is also a palpable sign of relief; nothing has been stolen from him. He takes his feet from the plastic chair that he moved from next to him and pushes it in front of him, this is the chair that he used to rest his legs on, then he moves the chair back to the position that it was in originally. He bends over and looks beneath the chair on which he still sits, both of his bags are there, he looks closer, the padlock is still fastened, neither the suitcase nor the computer bag has been cut through with a knife. He wipes his hand across his mouth, *bile, death is always sweet, waking is to be alive, remove the body from the bliss of death, sacrifice yourself to reality, I am a sacrificial discourse, bile is never sweet*, then he takes the handkerchief, the handkerchief that he used to dry his face in the bathroom, the same handkerchief that the man beside him, the man beside him in the mirror, used to wipe water from his face, and wipes his eyes, *the true grit of sleep, boulders stop the light, but light is never bright, it flickers.* One hour is a long time to sleep upright in a chair in the airport although many people do this, around him at least half a dozen people, old and young, men and women, all sleep, the man two chairs away from him has his mouth open and is snoring.

The sleepers are unaware of the activity and the sudden loud noise, the commotion on the television, the policemen running into the bar where Volker had previously been in to drink his beer and smoke a cigarette. Barricades, *I am toughly woken.* People are corralled, *cows become beef.* Volker looks around him at the commotion, at the noise, *war erupting,* the myriad people in uniforms, frightened faces of children *in an abattoir.* In front of him on a television a woman with blonde hair and blue eyes peers out at him from the screen. *I have seen her before, she is a clone, the world despises a world in which human beings are manufactured, we are all manufactured, mass-produced, let us make clones of happy people, no colour people, no gender people, hairless clowns, I am a sheep.* She is dressed in immodest clothing for winter, a short black skirt that does not cover her knees, thin black stockings, a white jersey vest, the snowflakes whorl around her, it is hot inside Terminal 1, the air is kept at a constant temperature, all through the day, all through the night, for the airport never closes, the airport is never motionless, there is always someone arriving, someone leaving, someone moving to somewhere. The woman, *a woman or an emulation, alive or dead, is that a button beneath her earlobe, switch it on, switch it off, a doll-like musical pageant, Ophelia is dying,* with the blonde hair and blue eyes that looks from the television screen seems to be looking at him, at him alone. *She stares with eyes of glass, will a blue eye always be a glass eye,* she seems unconcerned that there are many people around him, sleeping people, awake people, *people who notice the lascivious lick of a lip, the touch of a fingertip, she locates him with a counterfeit smile,* she has no need to look at those that sleep, they cannot look at her, but the many who are awake, those that walk now with fear for they do not know why their travel plans have been thwarted, *I am dismissed for a higher cause, insignificance, why there is such movement,* such activity, *faces vexed with exhaustion* to and from the food outlets, the bars, who walk across the concourse to the information computers to try and find more information and the vending machines, *hunger dissolves fear, all fast food is fatty, there are many people that she could converge on but she focuses only on me, a camera lens, camera lucida, I am not here for you to remember, I am time gone by, a timetable of no importance.* She holds a microphone in front of her mouth and tells the world the world news. She holds the microphone so close to her lips that Volker can see the lipstick marks on its tip, *the lipstick marks surround my cock where the skin has been rolled down, a ring of fire at its head, will she warn me, the thought police are moving in, closing in on me, I have not taken my medication, I am tired, there is no focus but an eclipse, a moon, the sliver of silver, silver hair, the glazed edges*

of the whole envelope, the half, the new is engulfed by the old,
her eyes are blue, *cerulean contact lenses, synthetic happiness
is as blue as an eye, an azure alias,* her hair is blonde and her
mouth is red.

A barman of Algerian origin, *a deformed delinquent, he
does not speak my language, a patois,* has been arrested at
Charles de Gaulle airport in Paris, a DIY hydrogen detona-
tion bomb, ready to use, *could be made by anyone, even a
child of limited dexterity, so easy,* was stored behind the bar
counter at which he served. The 27-year-old man, *27 years
have passed since he was born, 47 years or more, or less, have
passed since the massacre of pieds noirs,*[42] has been arrested
after police found an automatic pistol, a machine-gun, five
bars of plastic explosives and two detonators in a cupboard
where people place their coats, *who needs a coat it is so hot,
a constant even temperature in the airport, subdued,* as they
come into the bar. Following the man's arrest the police
captured the man's father, his two brothers and a cousin;
*it's always all in the family, families hold the world together,
building blocks that fit together like Lego, a plastic nucleus,* in
a one-roomed flat in the north eastern Paris suburb Bondy,
*let's bring out the dogs tonight, paladin, bring out the dogs, hair
raised, tears of blood.* The Algerian has since been identified as
Mohammed Ibrahim Moosa, *tomorrow I, too, will be one who
no longer works the airport.* People interviewed have said that

42. The pieds noirs, literal translation: the black feet, are those of French
descent who were born in Algeria during the French colonial period,
1830 to 1962. The pieds noirs returned to France when Algeria, after a
long and bloody war, obtained its independence. They supported colonial
rule in Algeria, exploited those whom they perceived as natives and hated
the Algerian nationalist groups such as the Front de Libération Natio-
nale (FLN) and the Mouvement National Algérien (MNA). As a result there
were several massacres, in both Oran and Algiers, in which a number of
pieds noirs were killed by soldiers of these liberation movements. Some
well-known pieds noir are Louis Althusser, Albert Camus, Jacques Derrida
and Yves Saint Laurent.

they would never have suspected him as a terrorist, he was so polite, *and then everything that I have done, everything that I have thought will amount to just one person fewer in the airport, one person fewer in this airport that could be another.* He is a barman with a security clearance for many zones within the airport, the French capital's main international hub, *history is a postcard, there are changing scenes on the one side, an airport, a mosque, an airport, a skyscraper, an airport, but there is no particular memorable message on the back, come back to me the weather is beautiful.* The man was detained as he was walking across the bar, before he could reach the cupboard, a source close to French police said. An observant member of the public, a passenger in transit, a short statured man dressed in the clown's clothing, was the one who had saved the day. Clearly in some shock, the man with dwarfism, it has since been determined, told a news reporter that he had surmised the Algerian was on duty because, five minutes before, the man had taken his order for a beer but had not reached into the fridge to remove the beverage from it. Instead he had walked across the bar in the direction of the cupboard. The short-statured man had called to him but the Algerian either did not hear him (or perhaps did not see him on account of his shortness of stature) and failed to turn around. The very short passenger had then stood on his suitcase in order to lean over the bar counter and extend an arm to pick up a clean beer glass, as the other barman, too, was unattentive. It was then that he saw something he flagged as 'unusual' below the bar counter – this was later identified a weapons cache.

MOHAMMED RASHID NASSERI is employed at Charles de Gaulle airport as a barman. In 2001, when he first applied to work at the airport, he was employed as a cleaner. Those of Turkish or any other Middle Eastern origin, are never employed in managerial positions. They are always part of the lower end of the service industry, even if they have qualifications and experience. Mohammed is a chemist, and he has a formidable knowledge of the Koran and the French postmodern theorists. He can quote tracts of the Koran, despite not understanding Arabic, and Foucault. He can understand French.

When the airport's cleaning services were outsourced to a multinational company[43] Mohammed was retrenched – the company was making insufficient profit and decided to downsize – but, fortunately, a friend told him about an opening at the airport's Jolly Roger bar.[44] Mohammed needed to remain in the airport; it was imperative if he wanted his plans to come to fruition. So now he was a bartender.

Mohammed does not drink alcohol. However he did, prior to his job interview and in preparation for it, learn about different alcohols (much as he learned about Foucault or the Koran); different kinds of wines, spirits, beers. He is able to describe them perfectly, if slightly melodramatically. He did this in his interview for the position of bartender. The interviewers were so impressed with his knowledge and the vivid manner he had of expressing alcoholic qualities that he was immediately offered the job. Once the paperwork was complete they offered him a glass of champagne to celebrate his new position. He declined and said he was

---

43. Nous Nettoyons les Toilettes du Monde's headquarters are in fact in Mauritius, which is a tax haven, and it has branches throughout the world, including one in Ulan Bator.

44. There are many of these Jolly Roger bars. They are well known in Europe and America. There are, however, none in the Middle East or the Far East. The bar's name beside the entrance is clear for all to see – 'The Jolly Roger' in large red letters. Beneath the name, in a smaller print, are the words 'Come in for a GOOD Roger'. All of the signs and the words beneath them are in English regardless of the country in which the bar is situated. It is, after all, an American franchise and the world speaks American.

Muslim; it was against all his principles to drink alcohol. This had never occurred to any of the interviewers for although they knew he was Turkish, or Iranian, or Algerian or from somewhere there, they all look the same, they must surely be like Europeans and enjoy a glass of the real stuff. If not, then they are suspect and deviant, possibly Al Qaeda. Mohammed did not look at all suspect or deviant. When he revealed his religion to them and told them that never in his life, his life of twenty-seven years, had he touched a drop of alcohol, two members of the interview panel thought the company should take back their offer to employ him. He had failed to disclose an important fact; surely one of the requirements, or qualifications, of a bartender was that the person drank alcohol. They were persuaded by the three other members that the company prided them-selves on their diversity policies, even though they were an American company, and that it was good, if not admirable, to employ Mohammed, a Muslim, for although he did not drink alcohol his skill at memorising the different kinds of alcohol and his extremely vivid descriptions of exotic cocktails, not to mention ordinary beers, made him a wor-thy employee for the bar. And anyway he smoked, and the bar was a smoking bar which also sold cigarettes. So they employed him on probation and prescribed that he learned to describe different kinds of tobacco as eloquently as he could describe alcohol. He then gave them a demonstration on how to blow smoke rings in the shape of naked women, this was really impressive.

What the interviewers did not know is that Mohammed is the brother of Mehran Karimi Nasseri and that he is deter-mined to fuck them, the bar, the whole of the French nation, over and over again.

Mehran Karimi Nasseri, the man lost in an airport. His story was made into a blockbuster movie starring Tom Hanks, Hanks may even have been nominated for an Oscar for this role, but it is the movie that is known and remembered, and Tom Hanks, not Mehran. He is the text on which Steven Spielberg based his script, not a real person with real feelings or a person who sometimes needs to use the bathroom, and this is getting more frequent as his prostate is beginning to play up. On 26 August 1988 Mehran was stuck in Charles de Gaulle airport. He could not move out of it into Paris which is where he wanted to go. Initially Mehran said that he was a refugee, but unfortunately his refugee papers were stolen by another refugee somewhere on the flight from Istanbul. Years went by, years of bureaucracy and court applications and political bickering, and still Mehran lived in the airport.

As time passed he made quite a comfortable life for himself. He uses the washrooms in Terminal 1 as they are far cleaner than those in Terminal 2. Here the cleaning staff are trained well by Nous Nettoyons les Toilettes du Monde. They are more motivated and, most importantly, all of them, except for one, are women. It is well known that women prefer to keep things clean while men trash them. He sleeps in Terminal 1 in a bed that he has made up in the Business Class lounge. (This is kept out of the press because passengers who pay a lot of money to travel Business Class would not be happy to know that a homeless refugee of Islamic extraction uses the same facilities as they do without paying to use them; in fact he is there on the taxpayer's account because of bureaucratic ineptitude.)

Then one day it was agreed that Mehran had entered the airport legally. He really had had his documents stolen by an unscrupulous refugee, the theft was proved. But still Mehran had no papers, nothing to say where he was from, where he was going to. Who was he? He was a nowhere, no one person. There was no country to deport him to and no country for him to enter. He was in limbo. And there was no Virgil[45] to help him navigate this state. He remained in the airport.

Then one day Mohammed, Mehran's half-brother, came into Paris. He was free to leave the airport whenever he chose to do so but, unfortunately for him, his accommodation was a far cry from his brother's Business Class lounge bed. He did not have a sauna at his disposal or a massage chair. So despite being free his circumstances were pretty awful. He had to leave the airport every day, or every night depending upon when his shift was, to return to the Le Corbusier-styled modernist, low-cost housing, that never really worked as a social experiment, located on the outskirts of Paris. Here, in the high-rise apartment blocks of the *banlieues* mothers scream at their children in the stairwells, and dog fights, in which vicious pit-bull terriers fight against each other, are regular occurrences.

But Mohammed is here for a purpose. He did not so much want to get his brother out of the airport – he realised that Mehran was living relatively luxuriously compared to him – but he did want to teach those bastard French a lesson. He believed that the world we live in, the Western world, had taken upon itself values which include greed, commoditisation, spectacle, the traditional values of the free market and democracy. In it there is no place for the perfume of Allah,

-----

45. Virgil was a great Roman poet. His most famous poem is the Aeneid, the story, in verse, of Rome's founder. Virgil believed that the Roman mission is, under divine guidance, to civilise the world. Virgil's work has inspired many other poets, including Ovid, Dante, who cast Virgil as the poet's guide through Hell and Purgatory up to the gates of Paradise in *The Divine Comedy*, Edmund Spenser in *The Faerie Queene* and John Milton's *Paradise Lost*. In *The Divine Comedy* Dante's journey through Hell, Purgatory and Paradise is described. Dante is first guided by Virgil and then by Beatrice, his lost love. When he looked into the face of God Dante says at this high moment, 'ability failed my capacity to describe'. (Most writers are unable to describe even when not looking into the face of God.)

the sublime fragrance of the angels, except as commodities; it is a world where money is valuable not for what it can buy but for what it is. This is a world of keeping ahead (ahead of what?) and keeping pace (with whom?), a world of competition and new management and very little poetry for, Mohammed realised this, it is difficult to get the news from poetry, difficult to find out which war is on where, difficult to know who the richest man in the world is. So it is a world without poetry.

For many years Mohammed pondered just how to do this, teach the bastard French a lesson. His thoughts jumped from poisoning the cocktails that he served to travellers, to placing a bomb in the luggage carousel or just spending an evening urinating and shitting everywhere he could in the terminals. This he realised after a while was practically impossible as the terminals are never empty, and, for a Muslim, this is unclean, and anyway the cleaning staff, one of which he used to be, would just have to clean it up. And so Mohammed thinks and thinks and tends to the customers in the bar.

Then came the day he met a dwarf called Karl.

Mohammed did not much care for dwarves, not that he had any real acquaintance with them, but he'd always thought them somehow perverse, that G-D was punishing them for some sinful deed. Then he met Karl. Karl showed him that not only were dwarves devious, clever and lascivious, and sometimes dumb, in fact much the same as anyone else, but that this dwarf could help him actualise his plans. And as Mohammed could not pay Karl – he earned only a bartender's wage, plus gratuities – all he had to do was give Karl, and his numerous friends, free drinks. So in some ways he was fucking the system. He also hated the Americans, along with the French, and was pleased with this arrangement. He did not know that Karl was an American, not a Canadian as he had said, or that he was not in it for the money but for the fun.

Karl never revealed to his clients that he did not need

money. The higher the fee the better the product, is what people think, so he kept his fees high and where, in this instance he was working for a few free cocktails, he pretended that he, too, was a believer, that he, too, wanted to fuck up the West and all of its civilisation. And so Karl enjoyed his free drinks. And he liked it that he could fuck the French (fuck anyone actually) but as the French were at hand, why not them.

So Mehran continued to live in the airport and Mohammed continued to work in the airport and passengers continued to come and go and drink and use the ablutions and generally nothing changed. The moon rose and set and the sun rose and set and no one in the airport knew of either of these occurrences.

Mehran lived in the Charles de Gaulle airport for a long time. And, due to the Spielberg movie, for which he was paid $300 000 for his story, he was the richest homeless man in Europe. When he got to hear that Mohammed was there too (he fortuitously overheard a conversation as he was washing his hands in the toilets of Terminal 2A, about a brother who had come to the airport to find his lost brother) Mehran sought Mohammed out. He eventually found Mohammed in the bar. The brothers were jubilant. They were meeting for the first time. From then on they spent as much time as they were able together. This was not as much time as they would have liked as Mohammed was in the bar and Mehran had taken up the study of law. The Sorbonne agreed to put a live feed video camera and an Apple Mac computer in one of the airport's stores. The store was a popular one, selling books and curios. One of its employees even looked similar to a famous fashion and wildlife photographer, maybe it is really him, who had had a few books published and many photographs in European fashion magazines. Mehran therefore spent many hours in the store attending lectures, working at a desk that was put up especially for him to work at, talking to the shop assistant who liked to call himself Peter even though his name was Jim, the former wildlife photographer, maybe he really was one, with whom he became exceedingly friendly, about the pros and cons of smoking and conservation and alcohol and the art of Andy Warhol. Mehran liked the Marilyn Monroe screen print, one of which was on the wall of the shop, and his image of an electric chair, and Peter said that he was once Warhol's friend when, a long time ago, together with David Bowie and Iman, and quite possibly Jean Michel Basquiat, they played with real champagne on the edges of Lake Turkana in faraway Kenya.

Footprint into the store increased and so did its clientele. Many people were so impressed with Mehran' s perseverance and courage that they came into the store just to look at him, and as they were already there they also bought books and keyrings and stationery. It was a win-win for all.

Mehran, who was now a Facebook friend of Steven Spielberg, he had actually met him once, although Steven does not remember him, also thought that Spielberg could make a movie of Mohammed's anguish and despair. A movie which would gross huge profits, millions of dollars, as it would depict the life of a believer who lived in a modern social experiment, who worked in a bar, which was against all his principles as serving alcohol was a sin, and generally suffering for his lost brother whom he did not know. He did not realise that this was not the kind of movie Spielberg made for it was unlikely to be a big earner.

But they were happy – Mehran because life in Business Class was not so bad; Mohammed because he had found a new friend in Karl the clownish dwarf, and as a perk, many women, for Karl was a well-known flirt and womaniser. Women love the disabled, it appeals to their nurturing side, but because Karl cast off women as quickly as he fucked them, there were many who naturally sought out Karl's friend for comfort, he was not that dark after all.

But unfortunately we know what happened to the bomb. The only positive outcome (Karl made sure of this and it was Karl, after all, who pointed the terrorist out) was that the French authorities arrested the wrong Muslim. Karl identified Mohammed Ibrahim Moosa as the culprit, not Mohammed Rashid Nasseri, but then all of Islamic extraction look alike, and Karl, he was not a suspect, for who would suspect a person with dwarfism, particularly a clown dwarf (and he'd tipped the authorities off), and Mehran … well, by this time Mehran was a famous victim and neither the famous, nor a victim, can be evil.

The arrested man swore that he was innocent. This did not help him. He was sent to jail for a long time. Eventually he died there.

BE CAREFUL, BE *very careful, kill those ants, kill those drones, kill, kill Bill, I will eat you.* A source, who cannot be named for security reasons, *be careful, be very careful, kill, kill me,* said that the arrested Algerian was not known to be close to any Islamist group, *there is no doubt that he is a Muslim cur, the anti-terrorist police are pedigreed dogs, their coats well brushed and soft, silk is smooth,* Charles de Gaulle airport is one of the busiest airports in Europe, and *the man led his troops into the battle, a successful battle, the only successful battle, he put all his cards and only two rusty pistols in front of the foe, and they call him brave, alas does anyone know what bravery is, he was defeated,* in Europe, *events are always consigned to the trustee-ship of the imagination, the memory of Charles de Gaulle is not solid like a tree, a desk, a glass window pane, something that you can own, changeable in time, always undependable.* Volker must leave, he must walk away, away from this mess of hurrying security personnel, soldiers in uniforms, that look all the same, and sunglasses and large heavy guns, and passengers who look afraid, afraid as they are escorted meekly from their chairs, their tables, their short time space, the time that he must spend getting to Terminal 2C may be a long time, *time is disciplined, space is disciplined, activity is disciplined, conduct myself in a disciplined fashion for there is punishment, I will be late and miss the connection,* he cannot know this for he has never walked from the one terminal to the other before, or caught a navette bus, so he will catch the navette for there is no other way to get from Terminal 1 to Terminal 2C. He takes the pamphlet from the pocket of his jacket, the pamphlet that he had picked up at the information desk earlier, *was this where I saw the miniature man, a goblin, a dwarf, the sanctuary of the great, what does the small man want, where is he going to, the small imagine greatness, the average sized cannot imagine anything bigger than themselves.* Volker looks at the map of the airport, the Charles de Gaulle airport, there is a picture of the great man on the outer page, *free the French, I am in exile, a performance for I have given up life, I am dead, a character in the novel of history,* he takes it from his pocket, the pocket of his trousers for he no longer wears his green parka for it is hot inside this terminal, it is always hot inside the airport, there is a constant temperature, a temperate temperature so that a traveller will never know if it is winter or summer, if the snow has banked up on the circular highway that leads to Paris, or if those outside wear T-shirts and sweat, *the temperature is prosaic, constant, no contradictions, humdrum, small minds of small great dwarves, the ambient temperature is enjoyable, never a mutation, no circular ambages, I wish for the life on the purlieus which is probably what I have, imagination saturated with no thought, on the outskirts, never ending, a line that leads to nowhere, a double helix that takes me in a circle, walking the tightrope with never the possibility of a fall.* Slowly he stretches his legs, the sleep, *the not sleep,* has frozen his limbs, in his dreams he dreamed of the television set and the blonde woman with the blue eyes who uttered a sound, *a mad sound, part fury, part overwhelming enjoyment, part schadenfreude at witnessing the pain of the other, a bit part in a small theatre.* She spoke of a terrorist attack, *the blonde hair falling, soldiers marching, marching me, soldiers that exude the smell of power, I am powerful, I have no power to run away, she bends, she looks at me, not the eyes but the eyes of the belt, threaded through eyelets on jeans, lean forward, open the zip, please, please, I want to show you my new Calvin Klein underwear, you are an image, dolls, are not all doll, I am a soldier doll, let me stay, let me stay.* Volker holds the map of the airport far from his eyes, he has not taken his glasses from the pocket of the parka which lies across his knees, two young people, Mark Wahlberg and Kate Moss, *Calvin Klein underwear on the billboard in front of me, I wash my hands in the room that was the toilet but was the cleaners' room, brooms and detergent, the elderly woman lifts her skirt, she is not the woman on the television, blue contact eyes, blonde Garnier hair, Calvin Klein underwear falls to the floor under deft fingers, dirty underwear, a whisper, my cock in her mouth, a new growth, soft, memory is unclear, like the picture on the television screen.* Volker stretches his legs underneath the chair that he used to put his feet on when he slept before the chaos began, there is a space here. He yawns, he looks at the map of the airport, *lines on the page, red and yellow and blue, red lines walk away, blue lines shuttle off to catch a navette, yellow go nowhere, no one knows what they are until they are travelled, lines move across the page, arch, go somewhere, flying into eternity.* He looks at his watch, there are four hours before he must board the flight that will take him to Africa, the continent that is always the same, *a continent of endless possibilities, persecuted and prophetic souls, too large, an ocean, a separate planet, Africa, a geographical appellation for Africa does not exist,* different languages, colours, cheekbones, climates, time zones, *always the same.* He rises and attaches the computer to the suitcase that has wheels. He hangs the red jersey around his neck, it is a woollen scarf it is so warm but there is nowhere else that he can put it, then he consults the map again. He gets up from the chair and walks towards the flat escalator, *a contradiction, somewhere there is a contradiction, there must be a contradiction the bland even temperature, a flat escalator, escalators must rise, rise like his cock rose in the cleaning cupboard, while he watched the image on the television screen, a film, X-rated, his cock is sucked, a suckling pig, the blonde woman does not have silver hair, can I want two people, I must choose the second one for the one with silver hair is no longer, how can I choose the first one if I have found the second? What is love, where is it?* As he walks forward he glances at the television, the woman with blue eyes and blonde hair is no longer there. A small man, *a miniature man, the dwarf clown,* who stood on his suitcase and used his fingers to tap out a question, the undersized man speaks to a soldier, *I cannot hear him, he speaks a language that I do not know, a dwarf language, a doll language, an advertisement for a giant doll that can walk and scream and cry, confusion, the sign of a mind that thinks, that draws pictures and sees consolation.* Volker concentrates on looking at the map, *walk to the escalator, the flat escalator, stand on it, or walk should you be in a hurry, walk to the next flat escalator, stand on it or walk should you be in a hurry, then another, then another, in front of you will be the entrance to the navette bus station, turn to the left for this is where the buses that take you from terminal to terminal wait, do not turn right for if you do this bus which is not a navette will take you to the heart of the city, outside space, outside the warm temperate climate controlled building and it will be cold.* Volker stands up and looks towards the escalator, he walks to the escalator, he stands on it and it takes him forward, then he walks a small distance further and stands on the next escalator, then the next and each time he moves slightly further forward. In front of him are some glass doors, they are opaque so that no person will walk into them thinking that they are an open space, *frosted glass, no one except those who are unable to see*

*will walk through, smash the glass, cut their foreheads, open
jagged glass shatters and falls to the floor, serrations mingling
with blood, cherry-red blood filled with oxygen, farinaceous
motes dot the eyes, take me by the hand and lead me through
the doors of perception, just in case I am unable to see, smash
the glass, dis-colour the beige tiled floor, overtime, extra time,
more money, I did not plan for this, there will be no misfortune,
there will be no hope, close the doors so I can* see. Volker turns
to the left, the navette is stationary under the neon sign, the
neon sign has the words, letter and number, Terminal 2C – 2
minutes 45 seconds on it, as he watches the sign so the
numbers 45 turned to 44 then 43, he hurries, as all the other
people hurry, for if he does not he will have to wait at least
fifteen minutes for the next navette, the sign has, in small
print, so that he has to strain his eyes, the times of the next
navette and the next and the next, navettes for 24 hours, the
times of the navettes. *How much time will go by when he is in
Africa, how fast will time speed, a relative idea, Africa, a space
with no time, where time is always late, a pleasing idea but
there is no time, no time to wait, no time to imagine a place
with no time, the night is as bright as the day, daylight, day
time saving time, the airport always saves daylight, lacklustre
neon, everyone is yellow, citrate.* He looks at the neon lit signs
above the navette, the electrical mode of transport that will
carry passengers on a journey from terminal to terminal for
Charles de Gaulle is a large airport, *far too big for overweight
and unfit passengers to walk in, and although I am not unfit, or
overweight, or am I,* and climbs onto the navette that says
Terminal 2C, *not 2A or 2D.* He does not need a ticket, for this
navette is complimentary, there is no machine that will take
his money, *a gift from Charles de Gaulle, did he give a gift to
the students at the barricades, a gift to the Algerians?* There is
no conductor employed to walk the thin aisles to take his
money because the navette is free, *free as a bird with nothing
to lose.* There is a seat available at the window, the window

looks out onto a wall, a white wall that the neon has yellowed, the wall has a painting of trees on it, passengers look outside onto a grassy field. Volker can see a brown cow in the corner of the field and several more black spots, they are probably also cows, *age spots, black fungus grows outside the temperate climate of the indoors.* The navette begins to move, the cows move with it, *steel on steel, and the wheels of the bus go round and round and round and round, round and round, and the wheels of the bus go round.* The painting comes to an end, now on the wall there is a poster, a billboard, a picture of a woman in a little black dress, the dress for all climates and changes and ages, *the climate does not vary, the ages do not change, the 21st century will continue forever as it is, temporary, forever is temporary, is temporary forever?* The woman in the poster holds a black bag in her right hand, her lips are red, from her lips a balloon emerges with the words, *I am different, I am unique, I believe I am so different and so I appear as if I am more of the same, I am the same, always the same, different, Chanel.* Volker is unable to read the words for the navette has already gone past the poster, *this is my swan-song for I can fly, an aeroplane, words are decorative, they curl around a tongue.* Now the navette moves quickly past a blank wall, there is some writing on it, graffiti, but it has faded, or else the cleaners have wiped it away. Then the ride is over, a few kilometres, nothing that Volker could not have walked, or nothing that he possibly could not have walked for he does not know how far he has travelled, it could be extremely far, *Terminal 2C is the terminal for Africa, it must be far away, separate but equal, a different colour, the other, the other that is not Terminal 1.* Once again he reaches for the handle of his suitcase, the computer is still firmly attached to it, the red jersey still hangs around his neck. He stands up, the doors of the navette swing open, he leaves the bus; he is in Terminal 2C. There is nothing here that is the same as Terminal 1. There are people, there were many people in Terminal 1, and yet here the people are dressed in different colours, *red, green, indigo* and different materials, *made in China, beautifully gorgeous, economically sound,* dresses, pants, overflowing garments, there are no suits, there are no little black dresses and there is a lot of hurry. People rush everywhere, they run, *they hurry along the road to happiness or unhappiness, only the stupid are happy.* Volker stops walking just to hear the sounds, he hears French, he hears Spanish, languages that he does not understand, myriad languages. He watches a man who is dressed in a turquoise robe bend down to adjust the strap of a basket covered in white linen, as he does so the linen falls, opens, the basket is a cage in which there are twenty green parrots,[46] small and young, *just from an egg, an egg yolk that is now green,* green birds, *taxidermy, mouths wide open, scream-ing,* mouths that make sounds that he also cannot understand, *sounds of grief, they have no home, sounds of joy, enfeebled, without wings, I have left the place that is so familiar, so common, so tiresome, without wings I am as insubstantial as a dream.* He looks about him, bewildered. This area is so different from the one from which he has come, *ephemeral things these human beings, am I a bigot?* There, in Terminal 1, things moved efficiently, they moved slowly, *eerily, as all pale bodies are ghosts, the movement of command, craftsmanship.* Here in Terminal 2C things are scurrying, darting in the sea of black, lips smile and eyes laugh, limbs cower down in corners. *I am doomed to choose, to have chosen this terminal, why am I going to Africa?* He looks at his watch, the hours have ticked by, he will wait a while and then, when the baggage lines are open he will join them and check in his suitcase so that it will fly with him, fly in the safety of the hold of Lufthansa Flight 345. There is possibly only an hour, maybe

---

46. The African Grey parrot, which is also green, is from Central Africa. It is the most traded bird, after chicken, in the world. Because these birds are now endangered, they are very expensive.

more, to wait before the call for lines open. He looks about him, there is no place where he can sit and so he stands, he leans his back against a pillar, at the place where his shoulder is the white paint is beige, many people have leaned against this pillar as they search for a seat. His suitcase, with the computer attached to it, is wedged firmly between his legs; he can feel it press into his thighs. He looks around him; *business busy-ness everywhere.* Volker feels tired from merely watching the activity; *this is a perfect expression not of order but the need for order.* To his left, at a table in the corner of the space, between a café that is closed, although the neon sign that shines above the counter is lit and points to a picture of a rooster, a dead red rooster, and a bar counter where people sit and smoke, *the air above them is grey and pitted through with cloudy bubbles, strange that in this terminal, people are able to smoke,* sit three people, two adults and a child, *are children people, and women, are they?* Volker looks at the table where the two adults and the child sit, *where one person sits, a man as I am a man.* A man, *who is this man, I must have seen him, I know him,* stands at the edge of the café, he too watches the table where the man and the woman and the child sit. The sign above the bar counter reads 'No Smoking'.

WALLACE STANDS JUST outside the café where he does business. From there he can look inside without being noticed, and Wallace never wants to be noticed. Wallace is a trader, a trader in human beings. He always laughs when he's asked what he does. A trader in human beings, he always replies. And then whomever he has given this information to also laughs. No one actually believes that what he tells them is true. In most instances those who ask the question are either friends, or acquaintances rather, because Wallace has no real friends – unless you count a small brown dog of no specific breed, and his cat, a perfect specimen from Siam; the blue eyes always stare – but he does have many acquaintances. He meets them in bars, in the park where he walks his dog (the dog is cute and cuddly), or in the vestibule of his apartment block. He is always honest about his line of work. He does not believe that he has anything to be ashamed of; in fact he always refers to himself as being part of the service industry. He serves, he says, both the people who want to sell their children – and of these there are many – and those who want to purchase them, and there are many of these too. The one is in need of money and has none and cannot feed another child, and the other has money and wants desperately to feed a child (and educate it and grow it in their image). Who could refuse either of these two parties? It is not as if any one of them is getting hurt. On the contrary, both end up satisfied. He prides himself that he only trades with those who are responsible and worthy, the best families. He would never traffic in prostitutes, or sell a child for pornography. He buys and sells only from the normal and the reputable. And he always does his research thoroughly.

Wallace takes a cigarette from his pocket, then a box of matches from another one. He cups his hands around the flame as it flares up; he lights the cigarette and blows a thin stream of smoke towards the ceiling. Then he remembers, he is not on the streets, he is inside an airport, and inside it is a no smoking zone, so he extinguishes the cigarette even though everyone around him appears to be smoking. He watches a rainbow form in the dust, then as quickly as it appeared so it disappears.

He is here to make sure that the job goes down well. He never gets physically close to his clients. He watches them from afar. He only puts them in touch with each other. The money is given by the one to the other, the goods handed over. Wallace has his share deposited directly into an unnamed account in Zurich before he gives either one of his clients the address of the meeting place where the exchange will take place. Beforehand he briefs them on Skype or by email; he sends them photographs and videos. Wallace is extremely professional.

At a table in one corner of the café sit three people. There is a man who wears a cap that is on his head back to front (this seems incongruous as he is a white older man, not a hip-hop twenty-something), a woman who wears only black, and a child in red and white and blue. Each person is always told exactly how to look and what to wear; this is how they identify each other. On one occasion the buyer was in a wheelchair so there was no real need to request that he wore specific clothing, but Wallace did anyway as he does not believe the disabled should be identified purely in relation to their disability.

The man at the table has silver hair and an unshaven face. His eyes are blue. The hemline of the woman's black dress lies across the middle of her dark thigh. Wallace knows this because, although she is now seated and her legs are covered by the table, he watched her walk with the child across the concourse. And he has looked at many photographs of the child both with and without her. He knows that the woman's knees are not attractive; they are large and bony. He thinks it would be preferable if all women covered their knees.

This is a scene that Wallace has watched many times. Both parties are nervous. Only the child is not. The child smiles, unaware of the transactions that are happening around him. The child has not spoken the whole time Wallace has been watching them. He is ten years old; a self-contained child, he seems always able to entertain himself. His red shirt stands out, a colour that goes well with black skin, as the black dress does not.

Wallace watches the table in the corner of the café. He has positioned himself deliberately for he wants to watch the expressions on the faces of the three people as the transaction is concluded, or commenced, he does not know at what stage it has progressed to, for he has only just arrived and it is obvious that the three people at the table in the corner have been there for some time, at least fifteen minutes. Wallace does not know if they are seated where they are, hidden from most people, because they want to hide, or whether this just happened to be an available table.

The woman in the black dress that is slightly too short, for her, and for most people, places three silver coins on the table. This is not sufficient to pay the bill; this is the sign, a way of showing that the transaction has been concluded. The coins are heavy and marked by use. She stands up. The child looks up from the corner of the table cloth with which he has been playing and he starts to rise, but the woman looks at him and motions him to sit back down. Wallace cannot hear her words but he knows that she is saying goodbye. He also knows that we can all be bought; the price must just be the right price, and good bye is only two words. And she knows that soon the child will be well fed and flying to Namibia where he will forget about Paris and enjoy the beaches and, in all likelihood, learn how to speak German.

THE SIGN IN the café should be lit up with a small bulb, but the sign is not lit up because the bulb has been broken, smashed by an irate smoker and not replaced, *blindness is not darkness but a form of freedom, and yet there is no freedom in this terminal, people are chained to their activities, for some nothing is sacred.* Volker looks across the space, the man, the woman and the child; the man with the cap on backwards has silver hair and blue eyes, *Judas faced, a cliché*, and the woman wears black, *every love story is a potential grief story, who does she love, who do I love, what can I love,* and the child, he wears a red shirt, it smoothes itself around his young body, *nubile*. The man, he is the second white man, or third, in Terminal 2C besides Volker, although when he looks around him more acutely he notices that there are several white faces, they are merely drowned, covered over in the sea of colour. White is marginalised in this social space. The man is unshaven. Even from this distance Volker notices that his face is covered in short hair and that his eyes are blue, *why do I notice the colour of his eyes, her eyes are blue, no my eyes are blue, why are blue eyes so un-impeachable, his eyes make me feel pain, does this pain mean that I have not forgotten the flavour of her skin, her memory, is this pain the proof that I love? Her eyes are brown.* The child does not speak, he, for it is a he, is wearing short pants and has a tie around his neck; the tie is caught in the collar of his red shirt; it is blue. He stares at the man, he seems intrigued. *Will this will be the last time that I watch this scene, or maybe I am confused and in fact it is the first time, or the second that I watch it.* The child appears to be about ten years old; he looks to be a self-contained child, able to enter-tain himself, *there is no future without a past, I cannot imagine anything except as a form of repetition,* the red of the shirt stands out as a colour between all the colours around him. Volker stands and watches. Suddenly a table and a chair become vacant, it is at least three tables away from the table at which the man and the woman and the child sit. Volker quickly takes the handle of his suitcase, and walks across the floor, he wants to sit down on the chair before anyone else does, and he is just in time, as he sits down he hears the slither of rubber soles on the floor, a young man, or should he be called a boy, has come to an abrupt halt, he was aiming for the chair, the chair on which Volker now sits, aw fuck you, man, my space, the young man gestures to him, Volker shakes his head, the universal negation, he cannot be bothered to say the word no, there is no need, he is not intimidated to move on. The boy looks around for another chair but there are no other chairs at the table, all the other chairs have been taken. He has head-phones around his head, they bend over and around his silky shaven skull, but none the less Volker can hear the music, or the sounds, the shrieks and the grinds, *the unmusical sounds.* He can now see the table in the corner more clearly, he watches the expressions on the faces of the man and the child, he has to lean forward and put his elbows on the table if he wants to really see them, *are they hidden because they want to hide, is she with silver hair merely appearing to be in my memory, is my heart broken.* The woman places three silver coins on the table, this is not sufficient to pay any bill, Volker knows this for he has made several purchases in this airport, but possibly these coins are worth more than the paper money that he has in his wallet. She gets up from the table and walks away. She touches the child on his cheek before she begins to move. The child looks up from the corner of the table cloth with which he has been playing, he starts to rise, she gestures for him to remain seated, *you put two people together who have not been put together before, were they always together, take one away and what is taken away is greater than the sum of what there was. This, however, is not mathematically possible; I feel it when I imagine her.* Although Volker cannot hear their words, he knows that what they say are practised words, the words that the man with the blue eyes seems to say are between a father and a son. *I am going to the desert, it is a soulless place where only the sky is king, the blue sky that is never clouded, the sky can never be harmed, but you can be and so I must protect you. I, and you, will be surrounded by the soulless, and our souls cannot struggle for all struggles are intended to be lost.* The man leans downwards and kisses the child on the top of his head, then he walks towards an ice-cream machine. The child, who remains seated, stares after him. After about three metres the man turns around and looks back, the child still stares at him, as if he is unfamiliar with this new face, he will not remember him if he loses sight of him, his look is wistful, he knows that he will never see the woman again, and so must keep the man constantly in his sight, *erase your memory as I try to erase my mine, I want to be liquidated for the erasure of memory is surely a liquidation, the making of a nullity, remember to watch yourself forget, begin a new memory.* Where the woman went to Volker does not know, *what will I do, where ever I am going to?* The man with the silver hair returns to the table, he leans over towards the child and takes his hand, he bends over and whispers something into his ear as he hands him an ice-cream, the child smiles and wipes a hand across his eyes. The child does not cry, he has no tears for they have already been cried, *he is as cold as a razor blade, he will not cling to that absurdity called love.* There is a rattle, a, sound, Volker looks upward, for a moment he turns away from the table now no longer of three but of two, above him hovers a bird, a small grey bird, a silver bird. The bird splays its legs as it attempts to gain purchase on the wire that is strung between two glass lights, the lights illuminate in neon a lightened notice board that tells people what time their flights are due to depart, or possibly to arrive. The bird looks at Volker, it flaps its wings and flies towards him, almost aiming for his face, *will it peck at me, will this bird take out my eyes, my eyes that do not want to see,* then it flies past him, he can feel the whisper of wings on his face. He does not know how this bird flew into the terminal, it is not an exotic bird, it is a Parisian bird, not clad in finery as are Parisian men and women, but a Parisian bird nonetheless, from the outside, flying under the rafters, *the radar,* of the closed-in airport. *Vogel is love without the letter g, g for garnishee.* Volker looks at the bird. The child in the red shirt stretches out his hand, his right hand, the man with the silver hair and the blue eyes looks at him and then he too stretches out his hand. Fingers touch, intermingle, the boy stretches further than the man, then he leans forward, his face is close to the silver hair now, close to the rough unshaven face. The man whispers something into the boy's ear, then he gently removes the bird excrement that has fallen into his hair, he whispers another word, *vogel, love me, for I will love you forever.* Volker looks up at the bird that flies in

Terminal 2C, free to fly wherever it wants to go to. Its wings are small and yet outstretched, it flies onto a table and pecks at a crumb, the movement of a person that is nearby, the rustle of a newspaper, make it take flight again, it soars to the ceiling, *what is freedom, the freedom of this bird that is enclosed in an airport terminal, where, how, can it fly anywhere?* The bird makes a sound, chhhirrrp, and then it settles on a high pole and looks downwards. *Did Icarus mess with the sun god? Does this bird mess with the sun god, is that why it is inside this closed space as there is no sun inside this terminal? Will it follow Icarus into the heavens, is this airport the only heaven that this bird will know. Trapped; Icarus falls into the ocean and drowns; we all know that we are going to die, the bird does not know of anywhere but this terminal.* The man with the silver hair holds the boy's hand, the boy is smiling now, he laughs at something that has been said, he looks at a book the man has put in front of him and points to something. *Vogel, love, love can be met in so many different ways; it is free to fly as the bird is free to fly.* Volker watches the man and the boy, the boy looks at the man, he is entranced, in love. The man also looks at the boy; he is silent now for he, too, is entranced, in love. *I cannot love, I cannot think except in fragments.* The man, he loves his new son, and the boy, the boy, he loves his new father, and the new computer that he may receive sometime in the future. *Love is fickle, it will change, is it ever solid? I pretend to believe in it, maybe I will forget the silver hair and the crooked smile, maybe I will build another new belief in the sand of the desert.* The line at the check-in desk is long, so long that it snakes around the sides of the walls, *snakes, an oily snake,* across the cement floor. Volker joins the line, he does not look forward only down, he is almost there, in a while he will have checked his suitcase into the hold of the long, large aeroplane, he will only have the computer to hold close. In the line there are many people who speak his language, *vogel vogel vogel* he is going to a place where his language is familiar, the words will be known by him. *Is this why I chose this place, Namibia, a place that I know nothing about except that which I have read about in books, except that they speak my language?* The man in front of him carries what looks like a gun, a hunting man, he wears khaki, his moustache is gleaming, he licks his lips in anticipation of the kill, the woman next to him also wears khaki, *eat sauerkraut, sour,* her face is twisted into a smile that is bitter, her lips do not move as she leans across the man and asks him a question, the man grunts, he does not answer, for he appears indisposed to answer, or maybe he just does not deign to answer, *women ask such stupid, foolish questions,* she is not worthy of his consideration. Another man stands to Volker's left, he, too, has the look of a European, the master race if not the chosen, he lectures to the woman who is next to him, *all men are didactic, they teach women something about life that only they can experience, woman must learn, she must listen, she only knows of life's experiences vicariously, she must observe.* Next in line is the man who holds the basket that is a cage, it is again covered by the white linen. As he moves forward a man who walks by knocks into it, the basket jerks, the man in the turquoise robe curses, the twenty green parrots make loud parrot sounds, *only in Africa can a man travel with twenty green parrots, why is he here, where does he go, they are diseased, sick, lice, I am a bird in a cage, this is my cage, I scratch these lice so that I can bleed.* The man with the silver hair who sat at the table close to Volker has also moved into the line. Volker watches him, he takes the boy's hand and holds it close, he is in control now, the boy acquiesces, he knows that he is not in control and never will be, *red, green and purple figures all around.* Volker gets to the counter. He places his suitcase on the scale, he hands his ticket to the woman who is behind it, she hands his ticket back to him. Both are silent, no one speaks in the cacophony. The man with the green parrots has moved to another line, it is to the right of Volker, he argues with the woman at the desk, he wants to hand his birds in, his caged birds that will never be free, *never be free as the enclosed bird that circles the airport Terminal 2C is free.* Two airport policemen approach the man, there is a scuffle, the bird cage is wrenched from dark hands, the door to the cage snaps open. The tree birds walk out of it onto the floor. People are afraid of green parrots, they may bite, *for they receive words and imitate them, is a person much more than a sophisticated parrot?* A bird waddles over to where the man with the silver hair and the boy stand. The boy reaches down to touch the green parrot, it snaps at his finger, a small dot of blood appears at its tip, the child begins to cry. The green parrot moves away. Then all the parrots run wild, *wings are cut, Samson I will denude you of your strength,* they cannot fly. Men chase after them, the birds run, crouching beneath legs, hiding under tables, inside a popcorn machine. *The clipped wings, their death will be banal, but my grief for their loss will be unique.* Volker moves from the counter and walks again towards a seat, soon he will be gone, flying, in the air, as a parrot should fly, *I will parrot a language that I have been taught, I will never remember, I will go and never return.* Lufthansa Flight 345 to Windhoek, all passengers please proceed to Gate 54 for boarding. Volker gets up from the seat, he takes the computer and begins to walk towards something else, he walks to the right for Gate 54 is to his right, *to right the wrong, I reverse left and right a difference, I have unlearned, is it my fault, and so I leave these many years behind.* Volker enters a corridor that will take him to his seat on the aeroplane. He leaves the airport as he arrived.

I am alone.

Barbara Adair is a novelist and writer. *In Tangier we Killed the Blue Parrot* was shortlisted for the *Sunday Times* Fiction Award in 2004. Her novel *End* was shortlisted for Africa Regional Commonwealth Prize. She is a contributor to *Queer Africa*, both 1 and 2, and her writing, particularly her travel writing, has been widely published in literary magazines and anthologies. She is currently working with the Wits Writing Centre at the University of the Witwatersrand.

Printed in the United States
By Bookmasters